"Lemon!"

The man walking out the front doors, barefoot and clad in white linen, with his arms spread in welcome, set Lennon back on her feet a few paces. Oscar "Ozzy" Wilder had filled out his teenage frame with muscles that ripped along his exposed forearms and the hint of pecs that flashed when his half-buttoned shirt shifted. He'd added some tattoos that drew her eye, but only until her attention swerved up to his face. He still wore his dark, shaggy hair shoulder-length and tousled. The tanned skin was new. No more Minnesota pale. And had his jaw always been so square and sharp?

The once-gawky teenager she'd crushed on had shape-shifted into so much more than Lennon could have ever handled in her teenage years. Guess she'd been saved by maturity. But for what? To become a sacrificial lamb bearing memories of her unrequited love as she faked that love for the next—how long did she need to be *the wedding date*? How was she possibly going to do this?

Dear Reader,

Join me for a summer fling on a beautiful Grecian island that dreams are made of. My heroine has those dreams, but will they come true? Spoiler: Of course they will. But first, conflict. That's the part where she agrees to fake date her former high school crush who left her jilted at the prom.

I never did go to prom. Well, I was invited—I even had a pretty dress—but let's just say my date's former girlfriend interfered and destroyed that dream. We all have high school memories. Did you marry your high school sweetheart? Did you crush on the cute guy or girl who never knew you existed? Or maybe you were an orchestra geek who would rather listen to Bach than figure out the complexities of the teenage dating game. Guilty! I promise there will be no cliques or popular girls whispering terrible things behind your back as you read this story.

And now I invite you to dive into the pristine blue waters and get your romance on!

Michele Renae

HER BIG FAKE GREEK WEDDING DATE

MICHELE RENAE

ROMANCE

If you purchased this book without a cover you should be aware that this book is stolen property. It was reported as "unsold and destroyed" to the publisher, and neither the author nor the publisher has received any payment for this "stripped book."

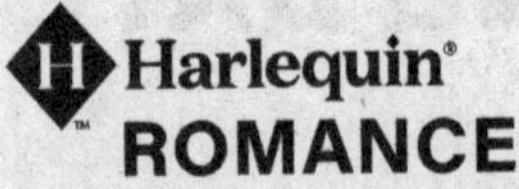

Recycling programs for this product may not exist in your area.

ISBN-13: 978-1-335-21702-8

Her Big Fake Greek Wedding Date

Copyright © 2026 by Michele Hauf

All rights reserved. No part of this book may be used or reproduced in any manner whatsoever without written permission.

Without limiting the exclusive rights of any author, contributor or the publisher of this publication, any unauthorized use of this publication to train generative artificial intelligence (AI) technologies is expressly prohibited. Harlequin also exercises their rights under Article 4(3) of the Digital Single Market Directive 2019/790 and expressly reserves this publication from the text and data mining exception.

This is a work of fiction. Names, characters, places and incidents are either the product of the author's imagination or are used fictitiously. Any resemblance to actual persons, living or dead, businesses, companies, events or locales is entirely coincidental.

For questions and comments about the quality of this book, please contact us at CustomerService@Harlequin.com.

TM and ® are trademarks of Harlequin Enterprises ULC.

Harlequin Enterprises ULC
22 Adelaide St. West, 41st Floor
Toronto, Ontario M5H 4E3, Canada
www.Harlequin.com

HarperCollins Publishers
Macken House, 39/40 Mayor Street Upper,
Dublin 1, D01 C9W8, Ireland
www.HarperCollins.com

Printed in U.S.A.

1 2 3 4 5 6 7 8 9 10 HDC 28 27 26 25

Michele Renae is the pseudonym of award-winning author Michele Hauf. She has published over ninety novels in historical, paranormal and contemporary romance and fantasy, as well as writing action/adventure as Alex Archer. Instead of writing "what she knows" she prefers to write "what she would love to know and do." And, yes, that includes being a jewel thief and/or a brain surgeon! You can email Michele at toastfaery@gmail.com, and find her on Instagram, @MicheleHauf, and Pinterest, @toastfaery.

Books by Michele Renae

Harlequin Romance

If the Fairy Tale Fits...

Cinderella's Billion-Dollar Invitation

A White Christmas in Whistler

Their Midnight Mistletoe Kiss

Art of Being a Billionaire

Faking It with the Boss
Billion-Dollar Nights in the Castle
Jet-Set Nights with Her Enemy

Fairy Tales in Maine

Cinderella's One-Night Surprise

Cinderellas in Seville

Match Made in Seville

Consequence of Their Parisian Night
Two Week Temptation in Paradise
Reunion with Her Highland Rival

Visit the Author Profile page at Harlequin.com.

To Jeff, because I will always remember the look on your face when you heard David Garrett playing AC/DC's "Thunderstruck."

CHAPTER ONE

LENNON HART FINISHED the edit to her latest TikTok post. Her *Manifest That* channel had fifty thousand followers. Over the past year, she'd taught others her simple method of manifestation by acting "as if" she'd already gained what she desired. It was like telling yourself a story. A person's heart believed what they told themselves. About literally anything—including the lies. It worked most of the time. Her sweet little apartment on Main Street above the local pastry shop was one such win.

After posting the Tiktok, she gave it a final watch:

Hey, Manifesteers! Lennon here with your Manifest Minute. I'm heading out on vacation so won't be posting Minutes but I will toss up pics of my adventure.

Remember how I manifested a real vacation to follow my brother's destination wedding? I've got two weeks to spend in Greece! And I've a manifest in mind for this trip.

If you've been following me, you know I've been working on my self-confidence. I can now perform a violin solo for a small crowd, engage in book club chats and even met the challenge of my first 5K race! But the last rung to climb on that confidence ladder is to put myself out there and attract love. Real love. Some of you can relate. I've had some fun relationships over the years, but I've never been able to step off the curb and embrace love completely. So here we go! Greece is all about the water, the air, the food, the sexy Greek men. I intend to manifest a hot summer romance!

Pause to flutter her lashes as if in a romantic daydream and give the camera a wink.

Yes, love is in my near future because I'm going to make it happen. In fact, the man of my dreams is already waiting for me as I board my flight to cross the sea. He could be in the airport. Waiting for a cab. Maybe we'll meet eyes across the counter in a tourist shop. Or he might swim by me on one of the gorgeous beaches. I've filled my vision board with tall, dark and handsome and lots of blue water and snuggles on the beach.

It's a done deal, Manifesteers. I'm going to

open up my heart to finding love! Thanks for following, and you can do it! Manifest your dreams!

Lennon nodded in approval. Manifesting such would finally erase that glitch in her self-esteem that wouldn't allow her to trust that she could have real and lasting love. She knew it was a story she told herself—that she would never find love—but that story felt real. She felt it in her bones. So to take a lesson from her own posts over the years, she was going to finally change that story by inserting a new belief into her bones.

Her flight was boarding soon. Just as she was about to switch to airplane mode on her phone, a call came through.

She almost dropped her phone at sight of the caller ID. "Ozzy?" Her heartbeat dashed into race mode.

"Lemon, hey, I've just stepped out of a Zoom call with a client so I have to be quick. You on your way to Greece?"

Lemon. He'd called her the silly nickname since that first summer he'd moved into the neighborhood and had become her older brother Harry's best friend. It had been a tease. And as an eight-year-old with a perplexing fascination with her brother's cute best friend, Lennon had at first hated it. But over the years, as that fascination had solidified into a genuine teenage crush, she'd embraced it as the special name only *he* called her.

A lot had changed since then.

Ozzy Wilder, host of Harry's destination wedding, had asked Lennon to arrive a day before all the family and friends started to arrive. While Harry's fiancée, Claire, had hired a wedding planner, Ozzy wanted Lennon to help him with some personal touches to the guest rooms because she knew her parents better than he did. Despite her reserved feelings toward him, and the fact that their only contact since she'd graduated high school had been the few times she'd run into him when he and Harry had gone on trips together, she'd agreed. Anything to make her brother's big day the best.

"Sitting in the airport right now," she said. Trying to slow her heartbeat. "What's up?"

"I'll get right to the point. Lemon, will you be my girlfriend?"

Lennon gave her phone screen a gaping once-over. Seriously? Those were words she'd once *dreamed* of hearing from Ozzy.

Yet now? Eight years too late.

What the heck?

This was not how manifesting worked. Ozzy hadn't even been on her vision board. Though certainly, he was tall. And handsome. Of course, she hadn't seen him in years. And that last time he'd been bundled in ski gear waiting for Harry after she'd dropped him at the airport.

His girlfriend? The last man on earth she would ever date was Oscar "Ozzy" Wilder.

Sure, she appreciated Ozzy for the solid relationship he'd had with her brother for years. But she hated him for those twisty feelings that always rose whenever his name popped into her brain. *He* was the reason her self-esteem glitched out every time the word *relationship* prodded at her.

All she'd wanted that night of the senior prom was a kiss. To have those words he'd whispered to her while they'd danced under the disco ball, *my girl*, to be real. To have years of swooning over the guy come to fruition with a dreamy moment of two mouths coming together in a fireworks-worthy validation.

The kiss hadn't happened. Because on the walk home following the dance, Ozzy had told her he had feelings for her—but that he wouldn't act on them because he didn't think she could love him. Something about his parents making him believe he was unlovable. As well, Harry's little sister was off-limits.

Her heart had shattered into a thousand slivers.

So now? She. Was. Over. Him. Because really? High school infatuation wasn't real love. And any guy who could leave a girl standing on the curb like Ozzy had done to her didn't deserve a place in her heart.

Thanks, universe. Way to dig up her most embarrassing moment at the very moment she'd thought to climb that last rung and own her confidence.

"What's going on, Ozzy? I thought I was heading to Greece to help fix up the guest rooms for my family. You know, rearrange a few throw pillows. Make sure the mattress will pass my mom's 'just right' test. If you're lonely and need someone—"

"I have a business situation," he said.

"A business situation? That involves you needing a girlfriend? I think that's called hiring an escort. I hear they're expensive. But you are a billionaire."

"Lemon, I don't need to pay a woman to date me. I need…"

His frustrated sigh had the weird effect of making her clutch her chest. The tenor of his voice had always given her heart palpitations. And not of the "see your doctor immediately" kind.

"A certain situation has come up and… I need to look like a family man, like I've got a good solid relationship. If you could pretend to be my girlfriend while you're here, that would really help me out."

Ozzy Wilder was asking her to be his *fake* girlfriend? She loved that trope in the romance novels but had never thought to find herself in such a wacky situation. Well. It wasn't going to happen. The last thing she wanted to do was to pretend to be in love with the man who had broken her heart.

"Lemon? Are you still there?"

"I'm…processing. I have questions."

"Toss them at me."

She did have questions, surely. But right now panic meant that she couldn't think straight. She wouldn't do it. She *couldn't.* Pretending to be Ozzy's girlfriend would be torture. So near, but perpetually just beyond her grasp. She wouldn't put herself in the same situation she'd been in as a teenager.

And yet… The idea of even pretending to be Ozzy Wilder's girlfriend did carry a strange sort of appeal.

Lennon shook her head. No way. She did not want to put herself through an emotional roller coaster with that man again. Been there. Done that. Hadn't bothered with the T-shirt.

But what if… Ozzy was the founder of the billion-dollar company Wilder's Wardrobes, which catered to the rich and famous with custom closets that were like dream homes in and of themselves. The guy was rich. He was also known for his bachelor reputation. Which meant…he had to have lots of single friends. Could he introduce her to one of those friends? Lennon was all about her dates being vetted by people she knew. And that would save time trying to *manifest* her future romance.

"Lemon! You're killing me with the long silence. Listen, whatever you want for doing me this favor, you can have it. I just need you to act like my girlfriend, show others that I'm all about family and have solid values."

"Oh. That's…" Ozzy had never come off to her as being family oriented. The little news she got about him from Harry lately was that Ozzy was winning in all aspects of life except for the family part. "Why me?"

"You're the first person who came to mind, Lemon. I was looking through some old photos the other day on my phone. That picture of us at prom popped up. And… I told the CEO of a company I'm bidding on that I was dating my high school sweetheart."

Sweetheart? *That* was his memory of the prom? Had he forgotten that he'd called her *my girl* while they'd been dancing under the giant disco ball? Yet only an hour later, he'd rescinded that endearment and had left her on the curb. Without a kiss.

"Are you kidding me?"

"I know! I never panic like that, but—I know

this is coming out of the blue, Lemon, but you *are* on your way here. Just name your price."

"I'm still thinking on that. On everything."

Could the man introduce her to the hot summer romance she was hoping to manifest? She couldn't avoid the fact that she'd put up a wall in order to protect her heart. Could facing her deepest hurt and resolving the past with Ozzy be the key to mastering that final rung on the confidence ladder? To finally opening her heart to love?

Seriously, Lennon? Don't do it!

"Just for a day?" she asked, the inevitable waffling of her inner strength kicking into gear.

"The CEO is stopping by to interview me. We don't have a definite date on when she'll be here, but it will be sometime over the next week. I figure we'll have to fake it the whole time you're here so all the guests believe we're a couple, too. Too risky otherwise."

For a guy who had panicked, it sure sounded as though he'd thought his through. "That's going to be a lot of work."

"You're the sweetest woman I know, Lemon. If anyone can make me appear as though I have family values, it's you."

She wasn't sure how to take that one. Was he implying she was not like those sexy model types she'd seen online that he'd been dating? She may not have the long legs and a curvy body, but she was…

Remember your goal: Be confident enough to manifest exactly what you want. Change the story you believe to something wonderful.

"I know what I want," she blurted out. It was the only way this could happen. "I need you to introduce me to one of your friends while I'm there. I want to manifest a summer romance."

"I, uh…"

"Take it or find someone else to pretend to adore you."

"Then I guess it's a deal. Thanks, Lemon. I'm sending a limo to pick you up at the airport. It's possible you'll be arriving the same time as my grandma."

Eliza Wilder? Lennon had never spoken to her, but she had seen her many times when Eliza had dropped Ozzy off at their house. "I'll look for her."

"Great. So, uh, if you're cool with this, then I think we're going to have to make sure Grandma believes were a couple."

"Oh." Heartbeat check? Picking up speed again! "This is happening so quickly."

"Grandma is not good at keeping secrets. When you see her, you'll have to play the girlfriend role."

She had always wanted to join the drama club

in school, but had settled for orchestra when one summer her dad had gifted her a violin. "I'm your girlfriend." The words didn't feel like English when she spoke them. "Got it. Ozzy, we need to set some rules before diving in too deeply."

"Agreed. We'll talk when you get here. There's the client I've been waiting on. He's got some important numbers I have to review. I have to go, Lemon. Thank you for doing this!"

The connection clicked off.

The intercom announced her flight was boarding.

Gathering her things, Lennon scrambled toward the departure gate.

So. The last man on earth she would ever consider dating had just become her fake boyfriend.

The universe was laughing at her. In order to find love, she had just agreed to fake date the one man who'd broken her heart.

"Manifest your way out of this mess, Lemon."

She'd never admit how much she liked it when he called her that.

CHAPTER TWO

THE SKY WAS some kind of blue Lennon could only place to paintings. The air felt fresh and clean. Most of the buildings were painted white, and everything screamed exotic locale that will subsume you into its aura and never let you go.

Loving it!

The limo driver pulled up before a luxurious property perched on the Ionian Sea. This was the island of Zakynthos, one of almost six thousand Greek islands. Lennon had looked up that figure while the driver had been extolling the virtues of Greece to her and Eliza, Ozzy's seventy-two-year-old grandmother. The woman who had taken him in and parented him since he was ten.

Lennon had found her waiting curbside for the limo. Eliza had hugged her and said she'd just gotten the text from Oscar that his girlfriend was arriving and to look for her.

"So you've come to enjoy the sea and sun a few days early, dear?" Eliza asked. The woman's sleek silver hair was cut in a chin-length bob, giving her a classic movie star glamour.

"You know it. Ozzy wanted me to help with some tweaking of the guest rooms before the whole family arrives."

"Oh, I do love to hear that you and Oscar are dating. I've known you for so long. Or rather, it feels like I have. Oscar talked about you so much when he was younger."

"He spoke about me?" A lump rose in her throat. What was that about? She didn't carry a single romantic feeling toward the man. Not anymore.

"Harry's annoying little sister is what he used to call you."

"Annoying? That tracks."

Eliza laughed, then pressed her hand over the back of Lennon's. "How did the two of you become a couple? Oscar is only in the States half a dozen times a year."

"We got together—" she'd been winging it since they'd gotten in the limo "—when he and Harry went on their spring skiing trip."

"Interesting. He never mentioned it."

The limo driver parked the vehicle, and then held the door open for them.

While Lennon waited for her luggage, she tilted her head back to take in the three-story ultramodern home. Fronted by groomed landscaping and lots of white stone, and bright pink flowers about to bloom. If architecture could be considered romantic, this was it in spades. Make that hearts. The perfect setting for a beach wedding.

Lennon snapped a shot of the landscaping, getting the beach and sea in the background.

"Lemon!"

The man walking out the front doors, barefoot and clad in white linen, with his arms spread in welcome, set Lennon back on her feet a few paces. Her breath woofed out of her lungs. Who. Was. That. Gorgeous. Man?

Forget gorgeous. He was…feastable. A full four-course meal. With dessert.

Oscar "Ozzy" Wilder had filled out his gawky teenage frame with muscles that ripped along his exposed forearms and the hint of pecs that flashed when his half-buttoned shirt shifted. He'd added some tattoos that drew her eye, but only until her attention swerved up to his face. He still wore his dark, shaggy hair shoulder-length and tousled. The tanned skin was new. No more Minnesota pale for this guy. And had his jaw always been so square, and…sharp? Edged with a closely trimmed dark beard. And a mustache that framed lips she wanted to—

Holy carp. The once-gawky teenager she'd crushed on had shape-shifted into so much more than Lennon could have ever handled in her teenage years. Guess she'd been saved by maturity. But for what? To become a sacrificial lamb bearing memories of her unrequited love as she faked that love for the next—how long did she need to be *the girlfriend*? How was she possibly going to do this?

Ozzy's eyes widened at sight of her. One strong hand rubbed his stubbled jaw. If the man had looked at her like that—was that…longing?—when they'd been younger, she may have melted into a puddle at his feet.

So over the guy. *And don't forget it.*

Ozzy suddenly cleared his throat and redirected his attention. "And Grandma!"

"Oh, Oscar, it's so good to see you!"

Eliza was swept into a hug.

"Grandma, I'm so glad you could make it for the wedding. Are those new glasses?"

Eliza touched the bright red rims and beamed at him. "My ophthalmologist said I needed some color."

"Beautiful. They bring attention to your bright blue eyes."

While Lennon took in the reunion with all the warm feels, she also felt an annoying tic creep up on her. The one that made her clasp her hands before her and bow her shoulders and head. Because no one ever noticed the nerdy girl with the glasses and braces who never got a date in high school. The girl who, despite her burgeoning influencer status and graduation from glasses to contacts, remained awkward.

"I enjoyed the ride here with your girlfriend," Eliza said as the twosome disengaged from their hug. "How come you didn't tell me you had a girl?"

"Ah, Grandma." Ozzy walked up to Lennon, and with a wink to her that Eliza couldn't see, he leaned in for a hug. A quick one. A little awkward because neither was sure where to put their hands. Ozzy slid one up her back and his chest pressed hers briefly. Was he nervous? Or as freaked out as she was about acting like she meant something to him? He whispered, "Thanks, Lemon."

If she shifted slightly, she would be chest to chest with him and— Mercy, he smelled incredible. But he pulled away quickly.

"Me and Lemon, well, we, uh…"

"Like I told her on the drive here," Lennon said, rushing in with the save. "We've only been seeing each other a few months. And long-distance relationships are a challenge."

"That they are," Ozzy said with a generous squeeze of her shoulder, hugging her body against his so that she stumbled into him. More of a brotherly hug.

Fine with her. In fact, they needed to agree that all physical touch should be classified chaste or she'd never survive the next few days.

"We're playing it casual this week," Ozzy said. "Uh, you know, not going to make a big announcement of our relationship, but not hiding it either. I mean, of course her family knows."

Oh, for heaven's sake, Ozzy. Her family did *not* know about this crazy farce!

They needed to put their heads together and come up with a game plan or this would never work.

"It's all about the bride and groom this week," Lennon offered. "We certainly don't need any attention on our little romance."

"Exactly," Ozzy agreed.

The slide of his gaze across her face battled with her desire to remain resistant to his allure.

The last time she'd seen him had been this spring. Idling in the airport drop-off lane, she'd been sitting behind the wheel in the car as Harry pulled his gear out of the trunk. Ozzy had waved at her through the open passenger window. She'd played her usual cool self, "nice to see you, Ozzy, been a while, see you later."

Was it possible to manifest indifference? While also pretending to be his girlfriend?

"Well, I'm delighted that you have someone

special, Oscar. I think it's great that childhood friends got together."

"We were never really friends," Lennon started.

"She was always the annoying little sister." Ozzy gave her a mock punch to her bicep. "Harry and I tolerated her."

"Guess you've moved beyond toleration," Eliza pronounced with a yawn. "Oh. That flight took it out of me."

Ozzy detached from Lennon's side, leaving her wobbling more from the experience of being around him than the actual physicality of their hug. He took his grandma's hand. "I've got your room ready. The one next to mine with the deep bathtub that you love. Figured you might want to take a nap on arrival. But only an hour. You'll never get over the jet lag if you sleep too long."

Had his voice always been so smooth? Deep and…liquid? Since he'd broken her heart, she'd maintained her distance from him. Easier on her emotional stability that way. He'd picked up on that over the years. It had been an unspoken line they'd drawn for reasons that neither had articulated.

"Oscar, you take such good care of me. But I don't want to be in the way of you and Lennon's reunion."

"I'm good!" Lennon called as she picked up

her suitcase. A moment to orient herself to this bizarre adventure was needed. "Ozzy and I will, uh, you know. Go on!" She waved them off.

Yes, please, leave her to process what had just happened. Gorgeous man had hugged her? Stirred up all the feelings she'd once had for him? Was she really agreeing to play his girlfriend? No—she needed to concentrate on manifesting her *real* summer romance. He was out there, waiting for a girl like her. And proving to herself that she *could* have a summer romance would mean that she'd be capable of a real love. So she had to focus and not get distracted by tan, ripped muscles. Gah.

"Help yourself to some refreshments in the kitchen," Ozzy told Lennon as he escorted his grandma inside. "I'll see you in a bit, Lemon!"

"Uh..." She raised a hand and waved a little. "Right back atcha!"

Lennon set her shoulders and nodded firmly. She was no longer that freckle-faced teenager carrying a hard crush on her brother's best friend. This week would be a business transaction. Both would get something they wanted. And that did not include each other.

But with one hug, would another be required? Just how far would they have to go to convince others they were a couple? And *could* she do that? Fake physical attraction to Ozzy without falling over the edge and plunging into the familiar but desperate longing?

Ozzy poured a couple of glasses of iced tea. He had not expected to be faking that he was part of a couple this week.

During a Zoom meeting with Amaris Chastain, the CEO of Cozy Closets, he'd thought she would accept his bid to buy her out. He had panicked when she'd told him they'd received two other offers. That they were reconsidering selling to him because of his family values.

Chastain had no idea what his values were. Yet she'd read the marketing blurb Wilder's Wardrobes had used last year, criticized it in a disdainful tone: *Bringing the sexy back to your closet.*

It had been a genius campaign. Ozzy himself had appeared in some of the ads, shirt off, leaning against the wall of one of their closet designs. Sexual overtones? Hell yeah. It hadn't bothered him at the time. And it still didn't. It was just marketing—it didn't represent the real him. Because in reality he was the nerd who liked to review profit statements and work the numbers, remaining behind the scenes unless the hired model called in sick for the photo shoot.

And Ozzy Wilder never panicked. He was cool, calm, collected. Always.

But it had been the judgmental tone of Chastain's voice and the way she'd rapped her fingers on the table. Really? Did she not understand marketing? That he'd been playing a role? The woman wanted to unload Cozy Closets. She should be happy she had a buyer who had agreed to pay the asking price. She'd known about that ad campaign before he'd submitted his bid. As well, she knew the history of Cozy Closets' inception. And still she'd initially agreed to his offer.

Yet when she'd mentioned the board had second-guessed her decision to accept his bid based on the possible clash between Cozy Closets' wholesome values and Wilder's Wardrobes admittedly sexual overtones, an unexpected hit of panic had urged him to blurt out, "It was just a marketing campaign. That's not who I am. I have a serious girlfriend. I am a committed family man."

That had piqued Chastain's interest. "Is that so, Mr. Wilder? Hmm..."

Cautioned by that long pause, he'd wondered if there was still bad blood between his grandmother and Chastain's mother, both of whom had been the original Cozy Closets founders. Would that be a sticking point? Sandra Chastain wasn't even alive anymore.

All he wanted to do was to buy Cozy Closets so he could give it back to his grandma. It had been Eliza Wilder's idea, her initial designs and a few important patents, that had founded Cozy Closets over thirty years ago. Her best friend at the time, Sandra Chastain—Amaris's mother—had partnered with Eliza, bringing in the initial cash. But five years in, things had gone south and Chastain had forced Eliza out and moved operations to New York. A noncompete clause had compelled a devastated Eliza to seek work in a different industry.

He could have bought out Cozy Closets years ago and added it to Wilder's Wardrobes inventory. He had the cash. Or possibly have sued them for property theft, but he'd had his lawyers look over the paperwork. Eliza had signed an agreement to release all ownership to patents.

Now with Cozy Closets up for sale? Ozzy wanted to pay his grandmother back for all those years of sacrifice she'd given him after he'd moved in with her following his parents' divorce. Eliza had worked relentlessly to support him. She deserved to finally get the company back in her name. It was the very least he could do to thank her.

He'd question his morals later. A little white lie about having a girlfriend wasn't going to harm anyone.

Lemon. His best friend Harry's little sister had changed. A lot. Gone were the braces, the glasses, even the zits. Lemon had been an observant bystander in his life. Annoying at times, in that she would often bop in and try to join his and Harry's Warcraft quests, or snoop in the garage where they would tear apart computer towers to see how they worked.

Spending time at the Hart home had allowed him to feel as though he had a real family. Had not been abandoned by his already distant parents. He'd been in desperate need of physical affection, a simple hug now and then. Hadn't been possible with his parents working eighty-hour weeks and Ozzy being raised by babysitters.

Lemon would beg for rides to school after Harry had gotten a fixer-upper Mustang for his sixteenth birthday. Sometimes they'd given in and let her join them—in the back seat, *and will you slouch down so no one sees you, sis?*—but most of the time, being two years older and *so* much more mature than goofy Lemon, who usually had a violin case slung over a shoulder, they'd ditched her.

Yeah, he'd always called her Lemon. Started as a joke, but it had stuck.

And very well, there had been times when he'd encouraged Harry to *just let her ride along with us, man.* Because there had been something about that goofy girl with the braces and bouncy ponytail. Something that had made it easy enough to agree when Harry had asked him to take his sister to the prom as a favor because she couldn't get a date. Ozzy had liked Lemon. And he knew she'd had a crush on him.

But at the time he hadn't known how to grapple with that attraction because—dating his best friend's sister? No way, man. She was off-limits. But as well, his heart had been trained to know that he was not lovable. So why even risk rejection with a girl who had meant so much to him? So after the prom on the walk home, he'd reluctantly dissolved Lemon's crush on him.

Now? Well. He knew Lemon carried residual anger over the whole thing. She'd been cool toward him since. No way, though, would he ever reveal Harry had asked him to take her to the prom. He never wanted to be the reason the siblings formed even an ounce of distrust for the other. So now he had to go above and beyond because Lemon deserved only the best treatment for helping him out of this jam.

Ozzy strolled through the living area of the vast three-story beach house he'd purchased after making his first hundred million, and walked onto the balcony overlooking the sea. The entire back of the house was trimmed with balconies, with a pool on the ground level.

"Is your grandma resting?"

He settled onto a lounge chair beside Lemon and handed her a peach iced tea. It was noon, and he had the whole afternoon ahead of him, but he recognized that Lemon and his grandma had already traveled nine hours and spent a full day awake.

"Yes. My housekeeper, Ilona, will wake her in an hour or so and serve her a hearty lunch. Then I've some activities planned to keep her busy but not overexerted so she can stay awake until evening before she succumbs to jet lag. How are you doing with the jet lag?"

"I've never flown overseas. So far, I feel fine."

Ozzy followed the stretch of Lemon's leg as she got comfortable on the chaise. Cutoffs and a T-shirt. Classic Minnesota summer wear. Her toes wiggled in the sea air even as she sighed and set back her shoulders. He recognized that opening up of the body. Every time he arrived here at the villa in June his body did the same. All his summers were spent in Greece. Of course, spring and winter were for Paris.

"All right, Wilder," she said, "what in tarnation is going on? Why am I suddenly your girlfriend?"

He'd forgotten she liked to use silly euphemisms in place of actual swear words. Cute? Definitely.

"Because you were the best woman for the job?" he said playfully. It had been that photo of them at the prom that had put her at the forefront of his thoughts when he'd panicked on the call with Chastain.

Lemon's suspicious gaze didn't buy his reasoning.

"I appreciate you jumping into the fake when you saw my grandma," he said.

"Improv is one of my skills. And I adore Eliza. But let's focus here. Why did I just agree to do something so outrageous—"

"I put in a bid to buy Cozy Closets. They're my biggest competitor. But Cozy is suddenly changing their mind about selling to me because they don't believe my values align with theirs."

"Your values? As in…?"

"Apparently I'm not considered family oriented. Or *cozycore*, as Chastain put it. It was one ad! But in real life, I'm not that guy from the advertisement who hangs around in closets, half-dressed, casting a sexy smirk at a model who is searching for her red dress."

"You're kidding me." Lemon faked a gasp, fingers to her mouth. "Here I thought all your closets featured a sexy man waiting for you when you walked inside. I am so taking that off my Christmas list. Aren't you the guy who brought sexy back to closets?"

"I did. Our designs are sleek, elegant, and you can almost imagine that sexy voice whispering to you when you walk in. Hell, you program the audio controls to just such a voice. But one clever marketing campaign does not make me a man without values."

At the time, posing sexy for the campaign had been just another marketing task. But when his dating life had also increased exponentially because of the ad, he'd gone with the flow. Nothing serious had resulted from those dates. Because really, no one wanted to fall in love with the boy whose own parents couldn't even love him.

"Chastain said something about me being a bad boy?"

Lennon started to chuckle, then abruptly stopped herself. "Well. I mean, it's kind of true. Advertising campaigns aside, I have seen photos of you online with beautiful women on your arm."

"That doesn't make me a bad person."

Having it slammed in his face by Chastain had made him question whether his marketing team had his back. They did, always. It was such a strange moniker to have slapped on him. Not even the few times the tabloids had gossiped about him dating a model had they insinuated he was a bad boy; just that rich guy who made sexy closets.

"You've got a very bad boy look, Ozzy. Dark, passionate and foreboding. Like every woman's most dangerous, uh…"

"Now you think I'm dangerous?"

"I mean, don't listen to me. I read too many romance novels. And it sounds like the woman is confusing a personal opinion with a business decision. But as for questioning your values, I've seen your closets online. They are masculine and hi-tech. Not something I'd imagine an eight-year-old girl with princess dreams sitting in and playing Barbies. They don't scream family man."

"The aesthetic isn't important. Nor is a genius marketing campaign that increased our sales exponentially. I'm a nice guy, Lemon. Not some shallow playboy."

"I know you are. Harry always calls you his better half—at least, he did before he met Claire. But I still don't understand how me pretending to be your girlfriend can help with buying a company."

"You're all about wholesome good values, Lemon. Your whole family is. Which is why I thought of you during the call with Chastain. And she let it slip that they were scheduling in-person interviews with the other potential buyers so…"

"Bother."

"I panicked. I countered to Chastain that I was all about family. And that I was even in a serious relationship. And maybe, since the bids were to be closed before the end of the week, Cozy's

CEO should stop by to interview me and meet my girlfriend. Then she'd see that I'm really a nice guy and she should take my bid seriously. Yes, it's a little desperate," he said. "But I need to tweak my image and prove to Cozy that they can trust me as the buyer."

"By lying to them?"

"I'm doing this for my grandma, Lemon. You recall that she was the one who founded Cozy Closets?"

"I do remember that. You told us about it one night when we were out in the backyard roasting marshmallows over a campfire."

The woman had an amazing memory. But so did he. "I seem to recall it was just me and Harry that night by the fire."

"Ahem. So I had a tendency to stalk you guys when I was young. You were always doing the cool stuff and I—" She sipped the tea. "Anyway, I remember something about your grandma's business partner stealing the business from her?"

"More like forcing her out and taking valuable patents along with her. All of Grandma's intellectual property remained part of the company. And while that's usually the norm in business deals, it wasn't as though she had a choice in the matter. Sandra Chastain used to be her best friend. And then they had some big fight and Grandma was pushed out. I want to get Cozy back for Grandma, Lemon. It would be a long overdue reckoning."

"Valiant."

"You think?"

"I do."

He hadn't asked his grandma if she wanted such reparations, but with Cozy Closets on the market, it would be a gift to her. A surprise. Eliza could do with the company as she wished. Whether she continued it through Wilder's Wardrobes or dismantled it was up to her.

"Don't forget you promised to introduce me to a billionaire."

"I seem to recall you asking if I had any single friends. Now it has to be a billionaire?"

She sipped the tea and wiggled her toes. The freckles on her face were copious and seemed to flow over her whole body…there were actually freckles on her toes. That was more than cute. It was downright adorable.

"Billions, millions, I suppose it doesn't matter. I posted on TikTok right before my flight took off. My summer manifestation goal."

He was aware of her influencing gig. Something about manifesting desires.

"As part of a yearlong series about boosting my confidence and learning to go for what I desire, I want to manifest a summer romance. That's going to ultimately help me to better open my heart to love." Lemon leaned closer and fluttered her lashes at him. "You must have single friends."

"Well, uh..." Lacking in confidence? She seemed pretty confident in what she was asking of him now. "Sure, I can do that. But the idea of having you play my girlfriend would not go over well if anyone sees you with another man."

"The introduction can wait until after the wedding, and after I've helped you get Cozy Closets back for your grandma. I've extended my stay a week. Tour the islands, do all the touristy stuff. I raided my savings to make it happen. So here's the deal: We play the couple, and get that company for your grandma. Then you pair me up with someone you trust."

"I haven't seen you in years, Lemon. You'll have to let me get to know you before I decide who would be your best match."

"I'm good with that. I mean, we'll have to do that anyway, right? But also," she continued, "can I post photos? It's necessary content to prove I'm here and pursuing my dream romance."

"Photos...with me?"

"No, silly. The beach, the shopping, all the glitz and glamour of living the high life will make for great content."

"I don't have a problem with that. But what if Chastain sees your posts? Glitz and glamour do not equate to wholesome and family oriented."

"Why can't a person have all of the above?"

Ozzy frowned. This had to go well or he'd lose any opportunity to win back Cozy Closets for his grandma.

"Does she have a TikTok account?" Lemon tugged out her phone. "What's her name?" She scrolled after he spelled the last name for her. "I'm not seeing her at all. Nor do I see Cozy Closets. And…let me just check Insta. Not on there either. I think we'll be fine."

"She could have an assistant?"

"If you let me post I won't show faces or allude to anyone that you're my boyfriend. My account isn't even under my name, it's ManifestThat."

"That should be safe then." He held out his hand for her to shake. "So it's an official deal?"

She eyed his hand far too long. Bit her lower lip as she considered it. She'd already begun the fake couple with his grandma; she couldn't refuse him now.

"Why does this feel so familiar?" she asked. From her tone he knew exactly what she was thinking about. Prom night. Him telling a moon-eyed beautiful girl that they could never be a thing. Damn. He'd make that betrayal up to her. He had to.

"I promise you'll get that summer romance, Lemon. And we can start… Is that all you've packed? Shorts and T-shirts?"

"It's what I have. You think I don't have the proper gear to play your girlfriend?"

"The best actress does need to become the part." And he could start making it up to her with a fun trip to town. "How about we run into town and pick up some things for you?"

Lemon's bright blue eyes sparkled. With a vigorous nod she shook his hand. "Fine. I'll do it. I'll…hold your hand and gaze adoringly at you. Call you honeybun. Giggle when everyone says we're so cute together."

"Honeybun? I don't know about that."

"Yet I get stuck with Lemon?"

"It *is* a term of endearment."

They bumped fists, and Lemon's gaze lingered on his for a few seconds. Sunshine twinkled bursts in her irises. Pretty.

She wanted a hot summer romance? Any man would love to date such a selfless, beautiful and talented woman. His admiration for her had not changed, save for that now she'd grown up and had gained more attractive qualities like the intent way she listened to him. And her willingness to set bygones aside and help him out with an urgent matter. Fixing her up would be easy.

CHAPTER THREE

THEY DROVE TO town in a Lambo. Yes, Ozzy owned a Lamborghini, and of course, it was a convertible. And, yes, Lennon felt like she had walked onto the wrong movie set and was trying to act a part for which she hadn't read the script.

"So how did we meet?" she asked. "You were visiting Harry and…hmm…"

"We finally gave into our long-held attraction?"

Lennon laughed. Did he have a crystal ball that could gaze into her soul? Yikes. No. Over the man!

"Yes, sure," she said carefully. "Long-held attraction. Works for me."

"Good. I think I saw that in a movie. It always works. We'll have to let Harry in on the ruse though."

"He'll do it. He owes me for so many times I've lost count."

"Same."

Lennon snapped some photos of the scenery.

"Will I have to talk to the Cozy Closets person when they stop by?"

"Would you mind? That's the reason I'm in this mess. I told her about, uh, you. You're so down-home, sweet and appealing. I think she'll like you. And if I can deflect her issue with Wilder Wardrobe's reputation to your appeal, then I'll be able to close the deal."

"You think I'm appealing?"

"Always have."

She smiled and wiggled on the seat. Ozzy Wilder had just called her appealing. Nice. But… "Oh, I get it. Right. We've got to play the part of boyfriend and girlfriend. So I guess I find you appealing, too."

"There you go. We can do this, no problem." Ozzy pulled into a parking space. "Let's get my fake girlfriend a fabulous new wardrobe."

While the town was small, it catered to the rich with high-end shops that Ozzy had insisted they check out. Lennon had tried on a few dresses and then when she'd checked the price tags Ozzy had tutted and grabbed them from her. He was spending thousands on her. And…she'd decided to let it happen. She was helping him out, after all.

Two hours later, she waited for Ozzy in the Lambo, using the time to put together a post. He'd said he had to run inside a jewelry shop to say hi to the owner. Could it be one of his friends that he may introduce to her when all the play-acting was done? She tried to get a glimpse of who he was talking to, but the sun's glare on the display window wasn't revealing anyone inside.

Her gaze fell to the bags near her feet. New clothes, shoes and swimsuits. She wrote a post on arriving in Greece. A few pics of the bikinis and sandals. A few more of the luxurious store-fronts. But the selfie of her sitting in the Lambo would send her followers to the moon. For the caption, she wrote: *Let the manifesting begin!*

She clicked *post* and tucked her phone in her purse.

At sight of the tall, dark stunner of a male specimen exiting the jewelry shop, Lennon sat up straighter. She touched her hair; the loose waves were trendy. So much she'd learned about pre-senting herself since high school. *Believe you are beautiful.* This fake would prove a practice run for when she attracted her own romance partner. Could she pull this off? Ozzy's girlfriend?

Eliza had believed their ruse. But then, she was over seventy, couldn't see without her bifo-cals and had admitted to Lennon on the drive to the villa that she wasn't hearing as well lately.

Ozzy slid behind the wheel and handed her a gift bag. "I hope you like it."

"For me? But I thought you went in to..." Talk to her future hot summer romance.

Well, who could resist a surprise from a jewelry shop? She pulled a box out of the bag. Flipping up the box top, Lennon gasped. So. Much. Dazzle. She ran her fingers along the black velvet on which a necklace nestled. "What? Oh, no. This is too..."

"It's perfect for you." He took the box and held the necklace out before her. "Let me put it on."

"But it's so..."

One gorgeous yellow diamond hung at the center, hugged by two smaller baguette diamonds to each side. The yellow stone was... Big. Bright. Sparkly. Like something a movie star would wear, but only for the night before the jewelry company demanded its return.

She couldn't possibly...

On the other hand. She was manifesting this week. And if one acted *as if* they already had the thing they desired, then other good things came as a bonus. She'd gotten the clothes. Was speaking to herself that she was beautiful. Accept it!

She pulled up her hair and Ozzy leaned in to put the necklace on her. He smelled like sea air. Mmm... Without thinking, she touched the ends of his hair.

Ozzy jerked back from her, his eyes darting away from hers.

"Uh, sorry. Just wanted to, uh…" She flipped her head around and ducked to look in the rear-view mirror. "Wow, this is a stunner. But I can't accept it. It must be worth tens of thousands."

With a chuckle he then said proudly, "It's a *lemon* diamond."

Like his nickname for her. Cute. But. "Is that even a thing?"

"Apparently so. You like it?"

"I love it," she said too quickly, then caught herself. "I mean, yes, it looks like something a billionaire would give to his girlfriend. Good going, Ozzy."

Of course, she would give it back after the charade was over.

"Thank you. Should we pick up takeout and head home to feed Grandma?"

"By all means, we can't starve Grandma. Take me home, honeybun."

As he shifted into Drive, Ozzy cast her a grin. And Lennon decided it was okay to like that sensual smile, even if it evoked deep feelings that she'd do well not to dwell on.

They found Eliza sorting through the kitchen cupboards. She was happy to see they'd brought food because she hadn't wanted to bother the chef. Now the threesome sat around the table, meals finished. The afternoon had grown into evening and Ozzy had seen his grandmother yawn more than a few times.

"When does everyone else arrive?" Eliza asked.

"Dribbling in through the week," Ozzy said. "The wedding planner doesn't arrive until the day before. I'm just the host, but the wedding planner has setups and deliveries arriving over the next few days, so I'll be overseeing those. The bride isn't making an appearance until the day before. Something about making an entrance."

"As one should," Lemon added with a regal wiggle of her shoulders.

The diamond necklace sparkled at her neck. He'd bought it for her spontaneously. Something inside him had whispered that she needed a sign of his appreciation for helping him out. And—fine. The teenager he'd once been had recalled how he'd left Lemon standing on the curb that prom night. Reparations were due.

When Lemon laughed and unconsciously touched the heavy diamond at her neck his eyes were immediately drawn to her. Harry's annoying little sister had blossomed into bright eyes, silken hair and a dazzle of freckles. She was lacking in self-esteem? Seemed to him she handled the role of girlfriend with an ease that only came from inner confidence.

"I begin cake duty tomorrow," Eliza said. "I've

got my plan and design ready to go. All I need now are the supplies, which I couldn't locate when searching your cupboards, Oscar."

"There's a delivery due tomorrow morning with all your baking needs, Grandma."

"Good boy." She patted his arm.

His grandma had sacrificed a lot to take him in at a time when she had just retired from the cake decorating business that she'd started after losing Cozy Closets, and had seen her a town star for her delicious fare. In her late fifties, she had been ready to head out and travel with her girlfriends, see the world. Not become a pseudo-mother to a distraught ten-year-old boy. Of course, she had never for one moment allowed him to believe she hadn't been thrilled to take him in.

"Would you two mind if I excused myself?" Lennon asked. "I'm feeling a touch of jet lag after that delicious meal, and if I don't swim it off, I'll be snoring before the sun sets."

"Of course, dear, you go." Eliza took her plate and rose but Ozzy beat her to it. "I've got it, Grandma. You sit."

The sudden side hug from Lemon startled him so he jiggled the plates. "See you in a bit, honey-bun."

"Back atcha, Lemon…drop!" He winced at the stupid addition to her nickname. Grandma didn't notice. He hoped.

"The day is getting too long for me as well," Eliza stated. "Do you think it's too early to turn in?"

It was only 6:00 p.m. The sun wouldn't set for hours. "Nope. You're good, Grandma. You've survived a long day of travel. Be sure to use the fluffy robe and towels I had the housekeeper put in your bathroom. You'll feel like you're snuggled in happiness."

"Oh, you're such a good one, Oscar. I do like that Lennon seems to be your opposite. Vibrant and a little kooky. She's not who I imagined you would end up with, but she's so lovely. How did you even go from being friends to, well…?"

Lemon would have jumped in with a great explanation. But, hmm…

"Last time me and Harry went skiing I took him back home a day early because he'd caught a cold. I…stopped in to visit with the Harts, reminiscing, and ran into Lemon. It was, well…we've always sort of had a thing for one another." True, in a manner. Not that Lemon had known he'd the slightest interest in her until he'd let it slip that night of prom. He'd treated her well, dancing with her, holding her close. Because he'd wanted to explore those feelings of attraction. Yet the few times since prom that Lemon had been in the Hart family home when Ozzy had been there, she'd avoided him or had left to go to work. Her cold shoulder had been well-deserved. "We finally figured it out."

How to break his grandmother's heart after the wedding? If there had been any other way to do this—but he hadn't had the time to think it through. He'd rushed into the first idea that had struck him without considering that it could hurt others.

But he was getting the company back for his grandma. No matter what.

"That's so nice, Oscar. I hope she's your happiness."

What even was happiness? Was it found in fast cars and big houses? No, those were just a means to get him around and a place to sleep. Running a successful business? That satisfied him. But as for emotional happiness? The idea of having a family loomed just out of his grasp. Having the Harts as an example had made it seem possible until he remembered that *his* family hadn't worked out at all.

His parents had divorced in a rage, both accusing the other of not supporting the other in their careers. Had they even bothered to consider how their only child had been affected by their indifferences toward the other? It had seemed so easy for them to walk away from him, claiming work demands, no time for hands-on parenting. Suggesting the other might like to take him. Ozzy had felt like the joker in a deck that everyone tried to avoid.

If his parents hadn't loved him, then how could he possibly find such love for his future children?

"This kitchen is yours to command, Grandma. Will you need an assistant?"

"Maybe. Ilona might help me?"

"I'll ask her." The housekeeper, who usually stopped in every third day, had offered to stay on the entire time the wedding guests would be here, which he appreciated. But he'd also hired staff to come in the day before and of the wedding. Everything needed to be perfect for his best friend's big day.

Ozzy stood and crooked his arm for her. "I'll bring you to your room."

"You're a dear, but I'm good. I'll see you in the morning, Oscar."

"Night, Grandma." He bent to kiss her on top of her sleek silver hair. The softest place for this boy's heart to land.

She strolled out and he grabbed the half-empty wine bottle. A glance out the window showed Lemon swimming in the pool below the second-floor balcony. Ozzy wandered out to the balcony and shaded his eyes against the glint of sun slicing the horizon in silver. Lemon floated, arms wide and eyes closed. The bright red suit she'd eagerly tried on when he'd said he liked the contrast of the white polka dots stood out in the blue water.

He'd had her suitcases brought to his room. Tonight he would—share his bedroom with her? Where was he going to put Lemon? He hadn't thought this whole charade through. They didn't have to share a room. Eliza, situated in the room next to his, was the only one who might see they did not share a room. And the majority of guests didn't arrive until two days before the wedding.

On the other hand, if he were to convince Cozy that he was in this relationship for real, he'd best get close enough to Lemon to make it look good. Which didn't require they share the bed. He'd sleep on the chaise in the closet.

Lemon stood, her shoulders out of the water, and waved to him. "This is amazing! I love Greece!"

He lifted the wine bottle to her. "You're manifesting it all!"

"Oh yeah." With that, she dived, her feet kicking out of the water.

Ozzy's smile overwhelmed his face as he strolled down the stairs and sat on the bottom step overlooking the patio. Life felt a little brighter today. His favorite grandma was here. And now, Lemon had bounced into his space. He was bound to feel happy when she flashed him her megawatt smile. And those freckles were like joy sprinkles. He was going to have fun the next few days.

Such hope-filled optimism wasn't new to him. He'd used it to create a billion-dollar empire. Not alone; he'd had a lot of expert professionals in his arsenal. But the *fun* part had been missing from his life. All work and only the rare play when he dated. He'd tried to enjoy those short-lived relationships, but work had always kept him distracted. Or that was the excuse he had gone with. Yet now?

Ozzy Wilder craved the laughter and light Lemon had brought into his house.

After some laps, Lemon sat up on the pool edge about five feet from him.

"I assume you're turning in early?" he asked.

"I've been yawning like a yak. You?"

"I usually stay up until midnight. The late hours are the best time to get some work done. My office is at the other end of the house, so I won't keep you up. I'll let you get settled in the bedroom, then sneak in after you're asleep. Promise you won't notice me."

"Wait. That room you brought my suitcases to is *your* room? I thought it was a guest room." She looked around, stunned. "I guess the closet was full of clothes. But, uh, I have to *sleep* next to you? Not so fast, Mr. Wilder. That wasn't part of our agreement. I…" She clutched her chest, suddenly seemingly…afraid?

"No, Lemon, I wouldn't ask you to. I was just thinking… People will wonder if we don't share a room. Grandma *is* right next door."

She pressed her hands to her hips, inhaled and exhaled deeply, processing. "Wow. I did not think this one through as far as I should have."

Same. "I can sleep on the floor. Or in the closet. There's a chaise in there."

Still caught in a stunned daze, she nodded while finally meeting his gaze. "Will we need to kiss in front of others to make our relationship believable?"

Ozzy studied her hopeful gaze. It wasn't so much worried now as…wanting? "I don't know. I, uh, I think we can get by with some hugs?"

She bowed her head. Nodded. "Right. No kisses. Of course, that should be a rule."

It would make things a lot easier if intimacy were not required. Because Ozzy didn't want to start feeling things toward this new and shiny girl—woman—whom he'd once crushed on. She'd confused his romantic heart once; he wasn't sure he could face that emotion again. The one that made him believe they were more alike than not.

"Good rule," he said. "No kissing. Just hugs.

We can play it up, make it look good. Hey, Lemon?"

"Yeah?"

"Thank you." He lifted the bottle to her in a toast. "I appreciate you doing this for me."

She touched the diamond necklace. "You're welcome. Getting to live a glamorous life for a few days is a thrill. But I won't forget you're going to introduce me to one of your handsome friends. Hot summer romance, remember?"

"I thought *I* was your hot summer romance?" he teased.

Lemon's jaw dropped open. The sight of worry filling her big eyes made him say, "Just teasing. I can do handsome. I mean, I think my friends are good-looking?"

"I'm not too picky on looks. It's personality that matters. How they treat a woman. Will they open the door for me? Ask me how my day has been? Slay a dragon or two?"

He had a couple of friends on the island, and one of them was single. Dimitri was a little older than him. He would be perfect for her. Hmm… Did he *really* want to introduce him to Lemon?

"I'm sure there's someone out there for you," he told her. "But I can't promise they'll be a dragon slayer. Good night, Lemon."

She waved. "Night!"

Ozzy held up the wine bottle as he took the

stairs up to the balcony. Here's to…a night spent on that hard chaise.

She didn't have to know it was uncomfortable as hell.

CHAPTER FOUR

LENNON WOKE IN the middle of the night and sat up on the massive bed. It had to be larger than king size. The luxurious linen sheets had welcomed her as their own. And the ultrasoft pillow had surely been crafted from kitten fur and clouds. Such was the life of a billionaire.

She glanced to her side and…the bed was empty.

She lifted her head. The massive floor-to-ceiling windows that overlooked the sea had something in them that adjusted to the light without need for shades. It was dark in the room but she could still see outside. So cool.

With a glance to her left, she saw through the glass doors of Ozzy's incredible closet that he lay on the long chaise placed in front of a wall of shelves. Aw. What a guy. Sacrificing the comfort of this heavenly bed for her? But really? She was a big girl. She wasn't going to jump him just because he was near and smelling sexy and…

How did a man get so attractive? It wasn't fair to females. To humanity!

Closing her eyes and curling onto her side, she smiled to herself.

But still reminding herself that she had been over Ozzy for years. Falling for him again was not what this smart, independent girl wanted to manifest. That last rung on the self-esteem ladder would be stepped on. She'd get that hot summer romance. And with hope, open the door to finding real love in the process.

It seemed just a little ironic that to get there, she had to fake date the man who had broken her heart and tattered her self-worth regarding intimate relationships.

It was no sacrifice waking in a huge bedroom perched on the turquoise Ionian Sea. Lennon had left the double balcony doors open last night, and the barest breeze kissed her skin. Yes, kissed. This felt like a fantasy cartoon where the heroine stretches, birds fly in to fix her hair, rabbits hop over with breakfast and the hero's teeth glint with a cartoon-like starburst when he smiles.

Nix the birds. She didn't want to deal with a seabird squawking over her head. And…bunnies probably hadn't delivered that tray of food sitting just inside the door. The scent of coffee lured her from the bed.

"Fresh fruit, pastries, orange juice and eggs? I am in heaven."

Picking up the tray she walked out to the patio and sat in her pajamas—jogging shorts and an Apocalyptica concert t-shirt—to dive in. Now if a hero walked in and his teeth glinted she just may pass out.

Lennon looked inside toward the closet door. No Ozzy.

Had to try.

Back to paradise. She could get used to this luxury living. But following the wedding she had plans to rent a hotel room in Zante, the closest town. She could hardly expect Ozzy to continue to host her while she dived into her quest for romance.

"Enjoy it while you can. Because all good things..."

Putting up her feet on the balcony railing, she checked her profile for comments on her post featuring the Lambo.

Greece? Wow! Nice ride. You manifested that? I am so following you, girl. Who was driving? Did you already find a man?

The dopamine rush she got from those comments made her smile. This nerdy girl was living the dream.

"Harry, my man!"

Ozzy hugged his friend at the curb outside the airport pickup lane. He hadn't seen him since their annual ski trip. Harry had always been the tech genius, the guy with the muscles yet quiet good looks. They were the same height, the same age, loved a challenging black diamond run, and always kissed and told. But only to one another.

"You're scruffing up with a beard nowadays?" Harry handed his baggage over to the cabbie who put his things in the trunk. They still had a ferry ride to the island where Ozzy's driver waited to pick them up.

Ozzy rubbed the neat beard that he was starting to like. "Gotta give the ladies what they want." He slapped his friend across the back. "How come Claire isn't arriving until later?"

"Claire is making a stopover in Paris with her maid of honor. A gift from her parents. She's calling it a premarriage vacation. Her last days as a single woman." Harry slid into the back of the cab and Ozzy followed. "She sent a dress there for some kind of fancy sewing on the veil. It was expensive, that's all I know."

"You can afford it with all the cash OpTech is bringing in."

"I'm not complaining. Whatever Claire wants, Claire gets."

"Good man." The car rolled away from the curb, and Ozzy pointed to the bar before them. He wasn't foolish enough to hire any old cab; he had developed expensive taste since building a fortune. "Did you have a good flight?"

"I can never sleep on a plane. I'm exhausted. Give me a shot of that brandy. That'll alleviate whatever jet lag I may be feeling."

"Or kick it into high gear." Ten in the morning shots? This week was to be a celebration of friendship, and Ozzy intended to live it up with Harry. Not that either of them were big drinkers anymore. He only filled the shots to the quarter mark.

Harry eyed Ozzy over his glass. "Why the shots, man? Who'd you make cry now? Or did she get you to buy her all the things and then left you dangling? Wait. Is someone pregnant?"

His friend knew that Ozzy had a manner of moving through women quickly. Hell, none had ever fully captured his attention. But he'd never fathered any babies. He wasn't that careless. Very well, he supposed his dating history did support the lacking family values label. He'd thought it just that stupid ad campaign.

Was he sabotaging himself by pushing away any woman who wanted to get even slightly close to him? Because he didn't want to deal with a future where he could follow in his parents' footsteps?

That was not him. At least, he didn't want that to be him. Even if he had decided to fake being a family man this week, he could really get behind a swerve in that direction. At twenty-eight, he wasn't getting any younger.

"No babies. Nothing dangling. You know I come from good firm stock."

Both men chuckled at the inside joke, a remnant from their teen years. They'd lived the wild life in high school and even when Ozzy had sought a skill in vocational-technical education and Harry had gone to the University of Minnesota, they'd roomed together. Some of the best years of their lives. Unfortunately, that *wildness* was getting old.

"I've almost sealed the deal to buy Cozy Closets," Ozzy said.

"Yeah? That's all I've heard you talk about since the ski trip. Your grandma will be so surprised."

"There was a snag."

Harry winced. "There's always a snag."

"Amaris Chastain, the CEO and daughter of the other original founder, doesn't want to sell to me because they are a family-oriented company. And for some strange reason they seem to believe I wouldn't be good for their brand."

"You mean the man who made closets sexy again by providing the option to install a sex toy section isn't allowed to sell ruffles and roses?"

Cozy Closets designed closets painted with

flowers, stripes and other juvenile interests focused on the younger set. In addition to the adult closets which, to Ozzy, looked like something a prairie wife would design, replete with actual fabric ruffles along the walls and roosters on the drawer knobs. Cozycore. It gave him a shiver. But someone was buying that stuff, so go figure.

"Apparently not. And we don't do a lot of those sections. Eh. More than most, probably. But in a moment of panic I told them I had a sweet, serious girlfriend and that family was what I was all about."

Harry hooked a disbelieving smirk toward him. "You? Family?"

His friend's doubt hit him in the gut. Did Harry also believe Ozzy was unlovable? The one person who would know that about him was the guy he'd spent most of his time with growing up.

Ozzy shrugged. "Like I said, I panicked."

"You never panic. Well, okay, you do when your best friend nearly gets plowed over by a sudden avalanche. That panic saved my life."

Ozzy lifted his fist and Harry bumped it. "Wasn't going to let my better half be taken out by a little snow."

"So did Cozy Closets believe you? About being a family guy?"

"I invited the company CEO to stop by to meet my girlfriend and see how family oriented I am.

I figure with the wedding and all the relatives hanging around that should be a sure sell. Will you back me on it?"

"Of course. I'm your wingman for life. So who's your current fling?"

"No current relationships. But I did find someone who agreed to play my girlfriend for the next few days."

"Sounds desperate."

"Harry. I need this. Grandma was crushed when she was forced out of the company. It was as good as stolen from her, and she's given up so much for me. I need to repay her."

"I get it. And I know how you've always wanted to show your grandma how much you appreciate everything she's done for you. So who is she? Let me guess—she's a model you met at a Paris fashion show? Or perhaps a professional mermaid, like that stunning chick in Vegas? I can't believe she made money putting on a tail and swimming in a tank! Wait…she's gotta be a redhead. You always go for redheads!"

"She's your sister," Ozzy blurted out. A wince was unavoidable. "Lemon was already flying in early to help with the wedding arrangements, so she popped into my head when I panicked. She agreed to play my girlfriend for the week."

Harry's mouth dropped into a gape. Then he

shook his head. Tightened his jaw. "Oh, hell no. You are not— Not my sister!"

"Harry. Chill out. It's just for a few days. We'll get our acts perfected for when Chastain stops by, and then we'll drop the act. Lemon is all in."

"Oz, you cannot date my sister."

"We're not dating," Ozzy said. Though the fact that Harry was so angry about it confirmed that the choice he'd made on prom night had been the right one. No way would he have been happy with Ozzy thinking it was cool to date his sister back then. "It's a ruse. And anyway, wasn't I good enough to take your sister to the prom all those years ago? What's wrong with me now?"

"There's nothing wrong with you."

Yeah? Tell that to the little boy who still took up space in his heart.

"And prom was not a *date* date," Harry continued. "You did it because I asked you to."

And he'd jumped at the opportunity to have that date with the girl he'd been so curious about. Man, he'd messed that up royally.

"Lemon agreed to do it," Ozzy added.

"Of course, she did because she's—"

"She's what? And she's getting something in return."

"Like what? Don't tell me you're paying her because that would be so skeezy—"

"She wants me to fix her up with one of my single friends. Lemon is in the market for romance. Hey." Ozzy held up both hands placatingly. "That was her deal. It's a business transaction between the two of us. I respect your sister, Harry. You know I do."

Harry's mouth compressed as he nodded. Finally, he sighed. "My sister is a big girl. She can do as she wishes. But really? She wants you to fix her up with some stranger?"

"He'll be fully vetted by me. I would never fix her up with anyone unworthy. Cross my heart."

Harry nodded, this time with appreciation. "This has to be the craziest stunt you've ever done, Oz."

"I'm already not proud of it. I hate lying. But I want to get Grandma's company back in her name."

"Eliza took good care of you, man. If you're doing this for her, then… I'll go along with it. But I'm not sure Claire will."

"I'm thinking we're going to keep this kind of quiet. Like we've been dating off and on for months and we're not sure we want to announce it this week and take away from yours and Claire's big day. So Claire can learn about it like everyone else. Trust me. This will work. Lemon and I will look like a pair, but after Cozy Closets have accepted my bid, it'll all go back to normal. And Grandma comes out the winner."

Harry sighed. "You get tangled up in deception, and nothing ever goes back to normal, buddy."

"Come on. I thought you were my best friend?"

Ozzy held up his fist and Harry, after a few seconds too long of a pause, finally confirmed their agreement with a fist bump.

CHAPTER FIVE

CLAD IN A floaty white-and-blue floral caftan—over a bikini, swim planned for later—Lennon breezed into the kitchen. The counters were piled with boxes and crates of food.

"Grocery delivery?" she wondered out loud.

"Kind of," a little voice called out. Eliza's bespectacled face smiled from between two boxes. "Good morning, sunshine."

"Good morning to you." Lennon grabbed a fancy bottled juice from the fridge and sat at the counter opposite a box Eliza was unpacking. She also wore a caftan, and over that an apron. "This seems like a lot of stuff for one cake."

"Oscar insisted I have top of the line equipment. I'm taking that mixer home with me. It is a beast!"

"Do you need help unpacking everything?"

"No, I want to go through and make sure I have it all. Oscar's sous-chef is also on call to help me. I know what I'm doing. I believe Oscar was looking for you."

"Where is he?"

"He picked up Harry from the airport and they wandered out for a swim. There's a big rock about half a mile out where Oscar likes to—well, I don't know what he does out there. Soaks in the sun. The man has a deep tan."

"Yes, he does."

Eliza tilted her head, taking in Lennon's sudden drop into admiration. "You really care about my grandson, don't you?"

"Uh, well…of course, I do." She tapped the necklace, still dazzled by its utter size and beauty.

"What is it about Oscar that makes your heart sing, sweetie?"

Lennon didn't even have to think. "I don't believe he's aware of his kindness. I especially love to watch him around you. He really cares about you."

"Oscar had a tough time of it growing up. I tried my best to make his life as normal as possible. You promise me you'll do the same? That's what Oscar needs is a counter to all this…excess."

"Oh." Lennon hugged the massive diamond against her chest to hide it. "There's nothing wrong with enjoying the money that you earn. It's not as if Ozzy spends it on booze and fast cars."

"That Lamborghini is fast."

"It is," Lennon agreed, propping her chin in her hand. Then she caught herself and sat up. "I should head out to the beach. I haven't seen my brother in months. A big hug is overdue!"

Leaving Eliza tapping her chin in thought, Lennon hoped she hadn't given the woman reason to suspect anything about hers and Ozzy's faux relationship.

And now that she thought on it, what would she tell her parents? She'd seen her mom less than a week ago as they'd gone over a list of items to pack for the trip. No boyfriend then. And she always told her mom when she was dating. Bother. That was going to be a difficult reveal.

And now she wondered when she'd have to perform for the Cozy Closets CEO. What could the CEO possibly want to talk to *her* about? Lennon knew nothing about closets. And if she were supposed to put on an act to make Ozzy look like a family man, well…

"I need to do some research," she muttered as she stepped outside and veered toward the white sand beach.

Lifting her hand to shade her eyes from the brilliant sun, she spied the speck of a rock in the distance. A bit far for her underutilized swimming skills. She would wait for them right here on the beach.

Harry and Ozzy swam back to the beach and Lemon met them with a playful splash of water.

Harry lifted his sister and tossed her a distance. She whooped and made like she was drowning. For a moment Ozzy's heart thudded with fear, until Harry nudged him. "She's fine. So dramatic."

In proof, Lemon stood in the water and stuck out her tongue at them.

Way to give him a heart attack. The last thing he needed was a drowning on his property. Or to lose Lemon. She splashed some sunshine into his life. As well, he was beginning to understand his younger self who had wanted to take her to prom to fulfill a crazy desire to get to know her better. On a more intimate level than his best friend's annoying little sister. Lemon wasn't annoying. She was radiant.

"Hey, Lemon, you actually agreed to be this idiot's girlfriend?" Harry said.

She shrugged. "I'm getting something out of it."

Harry rolled his eyes. "I don't like this at all, you know."

Ozzy wished Harry wouldn't keep rubbing in that fact. He already knew it.

Lennon balled up her towel and tossed it at her brother. "This business transaction is between me and Ozzy. Not you, Harry. So get off your high horse and play along, will ya, big bro?"

"My horse *is* high and it is a white stallion."

Harry made the motion of running his fingers along the brim of an invisible Stetson.

"My horse is a pony. And it's pink." Lennon made to flick off her brother's nonexistent hat.

"I'll have to tell Claire," Harry said. "She'll figure it out sooner or later."

"By that time the Cozy CEO will have come and gone. Just keep it under your hat, man." Ozzy tossed his towel aside and sighted the crew that currently hauled gear onto the main landscaped strip before the beach. "The guys building the dais are here. I'm not sure where would be the best place for it. What do you think, Harry?"

"I'm not good at this stuff. What do you think, Len?"

"Oh, boys." Lennon plucked up her caftan and shook the sand from it before flinging the garment over her forearm. "You've got to place it in the spot where all angles will provide the perfect photo opp. It's gotta be Instagram ready. I'd better go talk to them."

"You see? Leave it to my influencer sister."

"Thanks, Lemon," Ozzy said.

"No problem, honeybun."

Ozzy turned to catch Harry's smirk. "I didn't ask her to call me that."

"She's going to drive you mad before this wedding is over." Harry slapped the towel over a shoulder. "And you just might deserve that."

Was that so? So far everything Lemon did seemed cute and adorable. And he appreciated that she was stepping in to help with some of the things he had no clue about. How could that petite vision of bikini and freckles possibly drive him mad?

CHAPTER SIX

THE CHEF HAD helped Eliza find a place for her supplies. She was working over her recipe and ingredients when Ozzy stopped in to check on lunch. With Harry here he'd ordered pasta carbonara, which was his favorite. It smelled great. Ozzy leaned over the stove and inhaled the bacon-laden sauce. The chef nodded, never a talkative guy, but very precise in his methods.

"The wedding altar is all set up for maximum photo ops!" Lemon announced as she bounced into the kitchen. "Oh, it smells good in here. Hey, Eliza!"

Lemon gave Ozzy a side hug, arms wrapped across his chest and head hugging his shoulder. "Missed you, honeybun."

He caught her wink as she slowly extracted herself from him. But as she did, his fingers stroked her forearms sliding across his skin. His body reacted to her touch. He started to pull her back against him—then he remembered this was not for real. *Get it together, man.*

Seriously? That hug *stirred* something inside him. And it wasn't soft and smiley feelings for his best friend's little sister. Something *virile* lifted in him. And— *Stop thinking about it, Ozzy. She wants you to introduce her to someone not you.* Right. Because Lemon knew what family was and she wanted that relationship that would lead to love and family. All he could offer was a simulation of romance. Like fake dating.

His grandmother beamed at their embrace. "You kids look so good together. We'll be having another wedding soon enough. Would you ever move to Greece, Lennon?"

Lemon swung around the counter and sat next to Eliza, while Ozzy remained in place. This had just become a conversation from which he wanted to run. Because right now he was experiencing all kinds of unexpected reactions. Lemon in his arms had felt…right.

"I could definitely see myself in Greece," Lemon told Eliza. "And Paris! But we're in no rush with this relationship. It's still very new." Lemon cast a flutter of her lashes toward him. Cute. Yet that cuteness was also…sexy. Were those freckles *all over* her body?

What are you thinking, man? She's your best friend's sister!

And beyond that, Ozzy just didn't know how to make it last with a woman. Affection confused him. Was it false? Did she want something? Could he suck it all in and fulfill his desperate need for affection without freaking her out? Unlikely.

And to use Lemon and then toss her aside when he reacted to real affection and love? Not on his watch. She deserved only the best.

"I saw a red yacht out in the water," Lemon said. "Who does that belong to?"

"You don't know Oscar's yacht?" Eliza asked.

"Oh?" Lemon flashed him a worried look.

"I haven't been able to take Lemon out on it yet. That's the yacht I told you about."

"Right? Yours. Oh, yeah, we have to go out on that. Is that why it's up here?"

"The wedding party arrives later this afternoon, and I thought I'd take everyone out for drinks and a spin around the islands."

"I can't wait! Is that dinner?"

"It's called lunch." Ozzy leaned back as the chef plated their meals.

"Dinner," Lemon countered. "And later is supper."

"She's a midwestern girl, that's for sure," Eliza said with a snicker.

"I'm a midwestern boy and I've never called it that," Ozzy said. "Should we take *lunch* out on the balcony, ladies?"

"I'll join you in a sec," Eliza said. "Gotta freshen up and get this spilled vanilla off my sleeve."

"That's what I smell." Lemon leaned closer to Eliza. "You smell nummy."

Eliza laughed as she left them.

"Grab a lunch plate for your brother," Ozzy said as he made way outside where Harry was walking up from the beach.

"Dinner," he heard Lemon mutter behind him.

"Do you think she's buying it?" he asked as Lemon sat before the circular table. He was about to sit opposite her but was inspired to push a chair closer to her and sit.

She gave him a look that assessed but also approved at the same time. "Good move, honeybun. And, yes, your grandma is all in. I hate lying to her, though. She's such a sweetie."

"Just a few more days, Lemondrop."

"Do you give other woman nicknames when you date them?"

He frowned and took a bite. "I don't recall doing so. Why do you ask?"

She shrugged and her eyes widened. "So I'm special?"

Of course she was. Always had been. "You are enjoying your role, aren't you? You've been positively floating on air since you've arrived."

"That's the sea air and the fact I'm on vacation."

"Fair. I, uh…" Dare he tell her the sea air gave her a tempting blush and bouncy spring to her hair that he couldn't look away from?

Harry skipped up the stairs. "Food? Nice."

"I am enjoying it," Lemon said with a careful eye to him. "The vacation, that is."

"Ozzy's chef is amazing," Harry said as he joined them.

Ozzy nodded to her, a signal that he, too, was solidly in the role. Which was easier to assume than he'd imagined.

As Lemon grilled Harry on the vows he'd written for the ceremony, Ozzy studied her freckles. What was it, exactly, about Lemon Hart that still seemed to attract him in a manner no other woman had?

Faking interest in Ozzy for one senior citizen who was preoccupied by her cake baking adventure was easy. Soon though the entire wedding party would arrive, and then guests would start pouring in. And who knew when the CEO would stop by to closely inspect hers and Ozzy's relationship? A relationship that had a lot of holes in it. Lennon hadn't been aware he owned a yacht! She needed to up her game.

It was after lunch, and Lennon was uploading a video montage of the water, beach and the wedding dais. She added the caption: *Having the time of my life! Prepping for my brother's big day. Romance manifestation mode? Active!*

Then she checked comments on previous posts. Lots wanted to know if she had found a man yet. Many were debating that perhaps the Lamborghini belonged to her new beau. She could work with that. But hmm… She never wanted to be perceived as inauthentic. That was a promise she'd made to herself when venturing into this influencer adventure. Better not to reply to that comment.

"Lemon?"

"Huh?"

Ozzy's hair had its own personality. Tousled, sure. But also aggressively sexy. Like it dared her to reach over and run her fingers through it every time she glanced his way. Not fair.

"Are you doomscrolling? You know social media isn't real life. Everyone fakes it."

She set down her phone. "Not *everyone*."

"Your entire platform is about faking it until you make it."

"It's called manifestation. And manifestation is…a fluid concept. Sometimes it works; sometimes it doesn't. It's all about what the universe wants you to have, and you believing it will come to you. It's not like you wish for something and it magically drops into your lap. You have to clear the path to receiving it by inviting in all opportunities. Doing the work."

"Deep." He leaned back, kicking out a leg and the movement parted the white shirt that he only ever buttoned to his bellybutton. All that sexy tanned chest. With impossible pecs and abs. Also, that beard should be registered as a weapon of mass seduction. Mercy. "I just mean that a person shouldn't take the reactions and comments too seriously. You know? You don't believe that your followers care about you, do you?"

She did. They'd been with her for nearly two years. Some she recognized by their names. A few always remembered to send her birthday wishes, even though she never purposely announced it.

"Sorry. I don't know anything about influencing and social media stuff. I'll stay in my own lane."

"Thank you." At the very least he recognized that she may have some knowledge of her profession. A very fluid job that could be whatever its originator wanted it to be. "I'm just trying to…" Fit in. Be accepted. Live a life that did not require she work nine-to-five. "Make a living, you know? My sponsorships currently pay for utilities and rent. I'm doing well. But I still deliver for Hanson's Flowers to pay for extras."

"You can do it. You're talented, Lemon. Have you ever played your violin and posted it?"

She spun on the chair. "Never. And don't even say that I should."

Playing before familiar faces, mostly family members, was far different from putting up a reel for thousands, maybe hundreds of thousands to view and comment on. Lennon didn't have the fortitude for all the negative comments. She was well aware that some people lived to taunt others.

"Why not? If Claire thinks you're good enough to ask you to perform at the wedding dance, you must be talented. I recall you were first chair in high school. That has to mean you've got some skill on the strings."

When had Ozzy ever noticed the position she sat in the orchestra? Such knowledge would have been so far out of his coolness realm. "How do you even know that?"

He shrugged. "Wasn't like I never paid attention to you, Lemon. I've seen you walk home with your violin case hundreds of times. And the school orchestra did play at my graduation."

"Good ole 'Pomp and Circumstance.' We played at all the graduations. I love that song."

Knowing he knew that about her softened her defensiveness over his comments on believing her followers. "So, what's up for this afternoon, honeybun?"

"The wedding party will arrive in about five hours, and guests are going to arrive daily, as well. How about we relax on the beach before the storm rolls in? Give us another opportunity to get to know one another better."

"I'm in."

"Great. We'll walk down the beach to my favorite spot."

The man had a subtle smile that glinted in his eyes and made her breath falter. And her stomach jiggle. Pure sex appeal.

He winked.

Lennon had to swallow the giddy rise of desire that simmered right at chest level. *Do not sink back into infatuation. We're just playing a role, remember?*

The sea air had a way of making a girl forget about the small things that annoyed her. Like the swish of the caftan between her legs. The tickle of her hair across her face. The way the sand squished between her toes and stayed there.

Also, the fact that she'd told herself that she was completely over Ozzy Wilder. But was she?

The man who strolled alongside her, dashing to pick up the occasional shell or piece of driftwood and hand it to her for approval, was very different from that boy who had taken her to prom or who had ditched her a thousand times with Harry. He seemed more…in his body. No longer trying to impress anyone with the way he used to shake his head and smile as a hank of hair would fall over one eye, knowing it was girl bait. And quieter, even. He used to be a loud laugher and would always be the one, between him and Harry, to tell jokes.

Of course, he was being polite for her, perhaps? No, the man who strolled barefoot beside her, the wind blowing through his hair, truly seemed calmer. Settled.

"What about this one?"

The tightly spiraled cream-colored shell he handed her sported a pink blush. It looked like a miniature unicorn horn. "An alicorn."

"Alicorn?"

"It's what you call a unicorn horn," she said.

"Huh. Lost by a tiny unicorn, then. A fairy's steed?"

Lennon twisted an astonished look up at him.

"What?" Ozzy wrinkled up his face. "Don't you like all those fantasy movies?"

"I do, but I…" Never thought she'd hear the words *fairy's steed* come out of Ozzy Wilder's mouth. Rumored bad boy? Uh, how about sensitive charmer? "I'm keeping this one. In case its owner comes looking for it." She tucked the shell in the deep pockets of the caftan. "When is the CEO coming again?"

"Not sure. She's traveling to Paris from Dubai and she intends to set down here for a day or two."

"I looked up Cozy Closets this morning. They've got some amazing designs."

"Not as classy as Wilder's Wardrobes."

"Or as sexy. But a nice addition to your overall collection."

"You know I only want the company to give to Grandma. Whatever she decides to do with it works for me."

"Sure, but they are a multimillion-dollar corporation. They've been established far longer than Wilder's Wardrobes. Can't you just leave it branded as is and keep it as a spinoff of sorts?"

"Whatever Grandma wants, I'll do. But the fact Chastain is being spiteful about it makes me want to trash the entire inventory once I've got my hands on it."

"That's not cool, Ozzy."

"You say so?"

"I say so. And as your girlfriend I insist you keep Cozy. Market it as the other side of sexy. Or just focus on the family values. I have a theory about you."

"Do tell?"

"You like to believe you're not such a family-focused guy, but, Ozzy, my whole family loves you so much, you're like a brother to Harry and, er…" *She'd* never considered him a brother. Not when she'd dreamed of kissing him. "I'm just saying that sometimes a person tells himself a story, like I'm not *that* guy, and then that story becomes you. Even if it's not true."

"Deep," he said on a sigh. "Sounds like some of your manifesting stuff."

"It is. If you act 'as if,' then your body believes that. You tell yourself something, that's what it believes."

"Like you can't put up a post online for millions to see you playing violin because you don't have the confidence to do so?"

Touché. "Tossing the manifestation right back at me, eh?"

"I can be taught, Lemon."

Now for him to really embrace that he was worthy of the family he told himself he was not. Maybe she did need to post a short clip of her playing. Well. She had already progressed into opening herself to romance. It wasn't necessary to push too hard to the self-confidence finish line.

Ozzy stopped before a big stretch of driftwood and nudged the wood with his foot, giving it a wobble. "This is what I brought you here to see."

"A big log?"

"Lemon, come on, it's not *any* big log. It's my, uh, favorite log."

Had his voice grown a little softer? Lennon felt something akin to adoration for the man. As if the cute neighborhood boy had revealed a secret to only her.

"It's a very nice log," she said.

"You think I'm a dork."

"Not at all. Actually, it reminds me of a meme I've seen online. Something to the effect of, *since I've become an adult no one shows me their favorite rock anymore*. I mean, really, just because we're adults doesn't mean we have to completely grow up, right?"

"Not at all. And it's a very cool log. All twisted and bare of its bark."

"I like it." She patted the log's smooth surface.

Ozzy sat on the end and rocked it back and forth. "So can I ask about this search for a hot summer romance thing?"

"What do you mean?"

"Well, Lemon, you're a beautiful, talented woman. Don't you have a boyfriend?"

The compliment should have buoyed her, but instead her shoulders dropped.

Lennon could claim two boyfriends in her past. Both a good time and fond memories. But they hadn't clicked for the usual reasons. Very different designs on living in a small town as opposed to a big city. Also, who could possibly sit in front of a TV gaming all day long? That breakup had been bittersweet because he'd been cute and the only guy who had loved boba tea as much as she did. Also, she'd never trusted his frequent use of the words "love you." And in the end he'd walked away from her, leaving her standing on the curb.

That damned curb. It haunted her still. It signified loss of trust to her. Of never being good enough to win love. That was no way to move forward. But how to abandon that haunt when she couldn't seem to dislodge the very guy behind that curb haunt?

"My future boyfriend is on this island somewhere." Lennon stretched her arms and did a spin. "Romance manifestation, remember?"

"And you trust *me*, the guy who's never known real romance, to help you?"

"It was part of our deal."

But really, just because he was older and more handsome did not impart trust. *We can't date, Lemon. It would never work.*

"But if you want to back out," she said. "I mean, if you don't think there's a man who would want to—"

"Lemon." He put his hands on her shoulders. "Besides being beautiful you are kind and caring. Unique, too. And you would make any man the best girlfriend. So stop thinking that you wouldn't."

"Uh, okay?" But she'd not make *him* the best girlfriend. Only a fake one.

"I mean it." With that, he stood and started toward the villa. "You coming?"

"Right behind you!"

Yet she remained for a moment. He'd just shown her his favorite log. It seemed small, but clearly he was opening up to her. But her wariness was strong. He'd chosen the Hart family's love for him over dating her back then. And while it seemed commendable, what if they had tried? Given it a chance?

She glanced back at the log. *Why can I never kick you out of my heart, Ozzy Wilder?*

CHAPTER SEVEN

OZZY DIDN'T KNOW any of the six bridesmaids and groomsmen partying on the yacht's upper deck. As the best man, he was the outlier, having known Harry precollege, while the other men were all Harry's college buddies or business associates. He wasn't sure if Lemon was part of the wedding party. She hadn't mentioned anything. And he hadn't seen her whip out a purple gown as the other bridesmaids had cheered when a delivery arrived with a box full of dresses.

Leaving his grandma back at the villa, the group had swarmed the yacht and they currently floated in the Ionian Sea under the star-bedazzled night sky.

One of the groomsmen streamed his playlist to the speakers. The bartender kept the drinks flowing, and the top deck bounced with dancing and laughing bodies. Ozzy observed from near the bar, whiskey in hand. The women wore either bikinis or slinky dresses. The men wore shorts and tropical shirts like they'd planned ahead for some sort of goofy groomsmen uniform. One of them already had a woman draped around his neck. Were they paired within the bridal party?

If not? Ozzy smirked. Let the hookups begin.

Lemon was nowhere in sight. He would be able to pick her out if she were. She wore a slinky red dress he'd absently suggested she buy while in town yesterday. She'd grabbed it off the rack without trying it on.

At that moment Lemon's head appeared as she ascended the stairs to the top level. Like something out of a slow-motion music video where the vixen entered the room and cast her gaze around, the camera slowly panning up and down her body and to right *there*, where the low-cut neckline revealed the barest hint of cleavage.

Whew! Despite her petite form, she had legs that went for miles. Glossy hair that he couldn't tear his gaze from. That curiosity he'd held for her in high school returned, but with a new adult perspective. Harry's nerdy little sister had grown up. In high school if he'd walk by her in the halls between classes she'd flash him a big hopeful smile but then had quickly hidden her face behind a clutch of books. Yeah, she'd liked him.

And he had liked her.

Yet there was nothing special about him. Not now, and not in school when he'd been battling his own demons so hard it had been difficult to even see those around him. He'd almost been held back in fifth grade, which had been that first year he'd stayed with his grandma. Not for lack of trying; he just hadn't the headspace for math and English when his world had fallen away from him. The two people he'd once thought would always love and protect him had literally walked away from him.

At ten years old, Ozzy had gone to live with his grandma. His parents had never tried to contact him all these years. Not in person. His mom had sent Christmas and birthday cards until his senior year. Once one of the cards had been signed by her secretary, because he knew his mom's flowy signature. That messed with a boy's—man's—head. Because if your parents didn't love you, then who else could?

He did have his grandma, and the Harts. Thank God for them or he wasn't sure he would have accomplished as much as he had without them cheering him on.

He rubbed his palm over the tattoo on his forearm that read *Persevere*, then tugged his shirt sleeve over it.

"Ozzy?"

Startled out of his morose thoughts, Ozzy realized Lemon stood before him waving, as if to jar him from his thoughts. Could she see beyond his demons?

"Hey, Lemon. Good to see you out of the moomoo."

He stopped himself from reaching for her waist to pull her in. Feel her body against his. Run his fingers along that red fabric and find the places where it segued to skin. Forget that the world wasn't safe and kind and loving and just lose himself in Lemon's warmth.

"Moomoo? Seriously? I'll have you know, that was a caftan. It's very stylish. I saw a lot of women wearing them when we were in town."

"You pulled it off like a pro. It's just—I mean, you look…" He put up his hands. "Sorry. I, uh…"

"No worries. I didn't realize I had a body until I put on this slinky number. You really think it looks good?"

"Red has never looked better." What the hell was going on with his voice? Had he just *purred* that statement?

How was she such a good actress? And how to get on the same level as her and play along with the charade without losing track and feeling like it was reality?

"Thanks. I, uh, yeah. Thanks. So!" She grabbed one of his hands and placed it at her waist.

"Lemon? Are you okay?"

"Completely."

She leaned in closer. Wine and sea salt perfumed her. Ozzy closed his eyes to draw it in.

"I was talking to a couple of the bridesmaids as we sailed around that corner of the island," she said. "They were startled to learn we are dating. Because…well. We're not hanging on one another like we're madly in love."

Thus, the hand around her waist. Good call. The actress assuming her role. "In all fairness, I never *hang* on a woman." No, he just took them home, and…hoped they liked a good snuggle before leaving.

"Same. I mean, I'm not really sure I know how to hang on a guy." She wrinkled her nose. The disco lights dancing across her face competed with her freckles and the freckles won. "But we should try a little harder to look in love."

"Agreed, but it's weird."

"What's weird? Me?" She bounced to the beat of the music. A dip of her hip brought her down to eye level. "You don't want to touch your girlfriend, honeybun?"

"You know what I mean, Lemon." If she only knew how much he'd love to touch every part of her.

Seriously, Wilder? What was going on with him? Lemon was off-limits. And he already knew what Harry would think of him being with his sister—Harry thought he wasn't good enough for Lemon, and Ozzy knew he was right.

Lemon stopped bouncing. Sniffed. Sighed with a heavy drop of her shoulders. "Well, at least *I'm* in on the fake. You. Need to practice. Let's dance!" She took his hand, but at her tug he remained firmly on the bar stool. "I know you dance, Ozzy. We did it at prom."

"Give me one more drink to loosen up," he pleaded. And a moment to get his head around the fact that he needed to really do this. If he couldn't convince the wedding party that they were dating, then the Cozy Closets CEO would never believe it. "Then I'll join you. Promise."

"If you can find me!"

With that, she spun onto the dance floor and joined the others, fitting in as if she'd never shied from crowds when she was younger. Looking sexy and with it and so…alive.

Ozzy looked at his hand. He'd wanted to keep it there on her waist, his fingers conforming to her slight curves. Slide his palm up a little higher, under her tiny breast and…

And right now? That one guy with the blond hair was finding *his* place at Lemon's side. They swayed and shifted on the dance floor and Lemon spun before him, lifting her hair in utter joy and spreading out her arms. She beamed. And when the man slid a hand up her back to pull her closer, Ozzy stood.

Time to master the role of boyfriend.

Over the years, Lennon had learned to let loose. Or rather, to not care if anyone noticed her awkwardness. It had been a process, utilizing her "as if" manifestation skills. Since she'd begun posting online, her confidence level had not necessarily soared but it did have a noticeable rise. Also, it was easier to fit in when in a crowd. And the best place to let loose was on the dance floor. Loosing her hair, loosing her inhibitions, simply surrendering to the music and the happy vibe that everyone seemed to share. It didn't require manifestation to fit in with the crowd, just a little bravery.

With a spin, she winked at Harry, who danced with anyone and everyone. Her big brother was getting married! Way to go! Would it ever happen to her? Would she ever be able to open herself up to real love like that?

She hoped so! But first the universe intended to toy with her via the fake ruse.

The blond guy who shimmied up to her and touched her gently was cute. Connor, one of the bride's brothers. Raising her arms and twirling to the beat, Lennon turned out of Connor's grip and bounced right into a tall, stoic, brooding Ozzy.

Arms crossed and feet planted. He wasn't doing it right. Not the dancing part. And most especially not the madly in love with her part.

"You're supposed to move!" She danced before him, and when she held out her hand, he took it and dropped his stiff posture, assuming the beat.

He wasn't bouncy or erratic but had a sensual vibe that she quickly matched as the beat changed to something slower but still danceable. The overhead lighting strung across the deck jiggled, painting their faces in shifting shades. Laughter was mixed with beer, wine and hard cider. Yet Lennon suddenly wanted everyone to slip away and leave her and Ozzy alone on the dance floor. Since that would never happen, she followed the urge to touch him. To summon some of her Baby energy to see if she could get some Swayze out of him.

Drawing her fingertips along his abs, she walked around him, and then dashed before him, taking his hand and moving out in a twirl under his arm. He responded by snapping her back against his chest. Leaning forward, his cheek brushing hers, they swayed for a moment before the poke of another dancer's arm separated them.

Gazes locked, Lennon wanted to read so much more in Ozzy's dark irises than she suspected he would ever offer. That he cared about her. That he was attracted to her. That she was *his girl.* For real this time.

She'd manifested this moment. In acting confident and in her body. By not caring what others thought of her. And she'd been rewarded with his attention. An observation so intense she could feel it touch her skin. A hot stroke of desire skittered along her arms and up her neck.

But with a smile and a laugh, Ozzy broke that spell and twirled her again, swishing away the intimate connection.

She'd tried. Best to let it go. And stick to the ruse.

Lennon danced away from Ozzy and through the rest of the wedding party. Waving her hands before her to match the beat, she approached Connor. He had his hands on one of the bridesmaid's hips. Performing a spin, and splaying out her arms to get his attention, Lennon turned and landed—in Ozzy's arms.

"Oh." She initially pushed away, but when he held her firmly, she didn't have to force herself to play along. Her hips hugged his. Chest snug against his hard body. So difficult to decide if he were faking it or…

"You're mine," he said in a deep tone that had been polished to a rugged core-melting weapon. "Lemondrop."

With that, he dipped her. Actually dipped her!

Her back arched and his hand held her securely. No fear of slipping from his grasp. Lennon lifted a foot and stretched into the move. Surreal, and yet familiar in a weird way. She rose and snapped to his chest, eyes meeting in a sultry gaze beneath the stars. Oh yeah, there was his Swayze.

Rationally, she knew this was an act. *You're mine?* She'd heard that one before. *My girl.* But at this moment her heart wasn't in on the ploy. It tittered. It pulsed. It jumped in joyous exaltation as the heat of Ozzy's body melted against her skin. Her body went languid and she tilted her head onto his shoulder, curling her arms about him. A moment of intimate connection she sought to savor.

"How am I doing?" Ozzy's voice vibrated through her bones. Owning her. Marking her in a way she wasn't sure she cared to rub off.

"Five stars," she said. Then she leaned back to meet his gaze. "You think we've got them fooled?"

"You bet." He hugged her close and they moved slowly, as if a slow song played even though it had segued to a bouncy tune that had the entire yacht rocking.

Finding her place against Ozzy's shoulder, Lennon closed her eyes, and reached out for the dream of a hot summer romance.

CHAPTER EIGHT

AFTER THE YACHT DOCKED, the wedding party wandered along the beach. They were all staying in the guest bungalow down from Ozzy's villa. Ozzy walked alongside Lemon, guiding her toward the main house. He loved a good party. And it had been opportunity to take out the yacht, which had been in storage for two summers. But the quiet that lingered in the wake of everyone filing into the bungalow disturbed him. He didn't know how to do quiet.

Or rather, he didn't know how to be quiet with Lemon. On the beach. Alone. At night. Other women? Easy enough. Quiet meant time to make out, slip off their clothes and talk to each other with desperate kisses and seeking touches.

The red dress hugging Lemon's subtle curves was screaming at him right now. As it had when they'd been on the yacht. There had been no way he could have stood there and watched her dance with another man. He'd had to intervene. Dancing closely, they'd shared an unexpected moment, erotic yet reassuring. Like he was safe in her embrace. He could be himself with her.

He always had been, of course. But something had altered.

Lemon was not what he would call a friend. She'd been there on the edges of his friendship with Harry. Since he'd moved overseas, any personal details he knew about her had come from Harry. And yet, a gut-level attraction to her still existed.

As she wandered ahead of him, the red dress catching the moonlight with tiny flickers, he looked at her with new eyes. He was learning things about Lemon. It was different from when he'd dated previously. He never seemed compelled to talk and learn about a woman's history, her interests, or goals and dreams. Most never seemed interested in his dreams either. It had been strictly sexual. Nothing wrong with that.

Breaking the silence of the starry night, Lemon spun and laughed. At nothing in particular. She'd always been a little silly.

Lemon was what Ozzy had never allowed himself to be. Free. Uncaring what others thought about him. Owning her dorkiness with a seeming ease. Maybe he could open himself to Lemon's freeness and learn something from her.

At the outer door that led directly into his bedroom, Lemon stopped and waited for him to punch in the digital code. “Tonight was a blast. I’ve never been on a yacht. That fine seafaring vessel must have set you back a fortune.”

He laughed at her wine-influenced words. “It makes me happy, so it was worth it.” He opened the glass door and allowed her to walk in first. “Did you get some good pictures to post?”

“I’m going to go through them before I collapse in bed. So much great content!”

He knew he was just providing content to her. That had been part of the deal. So why did it hurt him now?

The look she gave him—was she checking him out?

Couldn’t be. That ship had surely sailed on prom night. Anyway, she was a few sheets to the wind, so he was not going to encourage any shenanigans when she was in such a condition. Not that she’d consider any suggested shenanigans.

“Uh…” She paused before the extra-king-size bed. Moonlight beamed through the windows, cutting half the bed in shadows, the other in ethereal light. A twist of her waist and she looked to the glass closet wall, behind which he would once again sleep on the chaise. “I don’t want you to sleep on the chaise tonight.”

Ozzy blurted out, “What?”

“I woke last night and saw you lying there.” She walked into the closet and plunked down on the chaise. Patting the velvet cushion to either side of her thighs, she nodded. "As suspected. It's hard as a rock."

"It's very comfortable," he lied. He liked the look of the leather chaise, knowing it wasn't for relaxing but rather served as a statement piece. He never imagined he would actually sleep on it.

"You were sprawled in the most uncomfortable position..." She flung herself down and twisted until her head was lolling off one side, arms flung out and one leg hooked over the opposite side. "Don't deny it!"

"Lemon." She stood, tugging down her dress hem. Slender thighs and perky breasts. Shimmy, shimmy, right into his desires, will ya? "It's only for a few more days. And if I really thought this was uncomfortable, I could have the housekeeper bring in a floor cushion. I've got something like that around here. In the yoga studio."

"You have a yoga studio?" She walked around him, arms akimbo, taking him in. "Who *are* you?"

"The designer talked me into it when I was having the house built. I can do a mean warrior pose." He quickly assumed the pose, then straightened. "But mostly I use the room to 3D print and store my closet models. It's basically an extra work room."

"Interesting. I assume this closet is your own design?"

"Naturally." He smoothed a hand along the cherrywood table behind the chaise. "I love the wood and brushed steel combination. Masculine but warm. And the glass gives it an openness that expands into the bedroom. It's me."

"It is. Except that part about being open. You've got a lot inside there—" she twirled a finger before his chest "—waiting to be discovered. Methinks that hard chaise is an example of your ungiving exterior." She tilted her head, considering. Then with a flourish she announced, "I've got to start gathering more data on you if I'm to make a convincing girlfriend. Our cover was almost blown tonight when those bridesmaids thought we were not a couple." She did a little tiptoe dance and bounced up to him. Bopping him on the nose with a finger, she said, "Honeybun."

Note to self: Keep an eye on Lemon when there was wine around.

Ozzy guided her down the steps into the bedroom. "I'm going to take a shower before bed, because you do morning showers, right?"

"I do."

"See? I know that about you."

She plopped onto the bed on her stomach, scrolling on her phone. "Well, I stand by my offer," she said as he walked toward the bathroom. "This bed is as big as your yacht. You can certainly take one side and we'll never touch."

"I'll consider it!"

He caught her startled gape, then laughed as he closed the bathroom door behind him. Lemon was in over her head. And not completely sober. And that made her more real to him.

That chaise *was* uncomfortable as hell.

Lennon woke in the middle of the night and looked toward the glass closet doors. They were open but the chaise was empty.

Twisting her head, she looked to the far side of the vast bed. Ozzy lay sleeping.

With a smile, she turned onto her side and fell back asleep.

Ozzy was not in the bed when she woke around seven. After showering, Lennon slipped on a soft violet dress that buttoned up the front and gently hugged her shape. The price tag was exorbitant. And really, how to wash linen? It involved special wash cycles and drying on the line. Being rich was complicated.

"Living the life?" she declared with some doubt.

She'd manifested this vacation. No reason not to go with the flow.

With a fluff to her hair, she decided to go with

minimum makeup. Her freckles would brighten under the sun, but she didn't care. After a smooth touch of her fingers over the diamond at her throat, she blew a kiss to the mirror.

On the way to the kitchen, she checked her stats. The reel she'd posted last night from the yacht—no faces of the wedding party and everything slightly blurred; she had a sense of personal privacy—was a hit. Comments were excited that she'd manifested such an adventure. And when would she reveal her relationship status with *that* man?

That man? Oh heck. She'd forgotten to edit out the selfie of her and Ozzy standing before the yacht railing looking toward the night sky. They looked like a couple, for sure. And anyone who saw it would think he was out on a lovely excursion with his girlfriend.

Had she seriously gotten drunk last night? It had been more of a fuzzy comfortable numbness.

She could take down the reel, but the commenters had already seen it. She didn't have to explain. Just another member of the wedding party. Or she could post that Ozzy was a friend of her brother's, but she preferred to keep the mystery.

In the kitchen the chef nodded to Lennon, asked her if she preferred a hot or cold breakfast, then proceeded to make her a delicious spread of eggs, meat, toast, cut fruit and a tall glass of guava juice. She took the tray out to the balcony, expecting to find Ozzy or Eliza out there, but she had it all to herself. The *shush* of waves called to her. That blue water was so clear, when standing up to her neck in it she could see her toes perfectly.

Stepping back inside to grab utensils, she asked the chef if he had seen Ozzy.

"Work," the man said bluntly. "Always until noon."

"Thank you."

The fact that Ozzy actually worked surprised her. Shouldn't he have a staff? People who did all the things that needed to be done? Who was she kidding? The man was the CEO of a billion-dollar corporation. Of course he worked!

Situating herself with her back to the water, she took a few selfies. Was her smile bigger than usual? Must be the sea air. Returning to Minnesota would prove difficult. Land of ten thousand lakes, give or take a thousand. Yet she rarely got to the cabin her parents owned up in the Itasca State Forest. Wasn't as though she was super busy. Her online presence allowed her to travel when and where she pleased. Her job with the flower shop was on call and only three or four days a week. So why *didn't* she take more time to get out and go on adventures?

"I need someone to go on adventures with."

It was no fun doing things alone. And her best friend, Maria, lived in the Twin Cities, a two-hour drive south, so they only saw each other about half a dozen times a year. Having a boyfriend would suit her pining heart. And provide her with an activity buddy.

But even if she did manifest a romance while here in Greece, it wasn't as though that person would follow her home to Minnesota. *Hey, kids, look, I brought home a Greek god as a souvenir.* Not.

"You need to find a man back home," she muttered. A sigh felt necessary.

She knew all the eligible bachelors in the small town of Tangle Lake, population six thousand and falling. Didn't have an interest in most, and the few she did were taken.

Expanding her horizons needed to happen if she were ever to truly make a life for herself. Which she interpreted as being financially secure, with a job that she enjoyed and making a family with a man she loved. Love, ever the goal. But there had to be a happy medium between Minnesota and Greece, for heaven's sake.

After she'd eaten, the chef popped his head out the balcony doors. "There's a woman in the foyer. She wanted to speak to Mr. Wilder, but he never receives visitors while working. I'd turn her away, but she asked for you. His girlfriend?"

"Oh." Handing the breakfast tray to the chef, Lennon said she'd check it out. Could it already be Miss Chastain?

The woman looked about fifty, with a chic brunette bob, wearing a fitted beige business suit. Her killer legs ended in black patent-leather Louboutin shoes. Playing the girlfriend of a billionaire was teaching Lennon to recognize the subtle signs of money that orbited him.

Lifting her shoulders and offering her hand, she approached the woman. "Lennon Hart. Did you have an appointment with Mr. Wilder?"

"Oh, you must be his girlfriend."

Lennon tilted her head as the woman's handshake was firm and sure.

"I'm Amaris Chastain. Cozy Closets. Mr. Wilder mentioned I should stop in as soon as I arrived in Greece. I've been eager to meet you."

"Right, Miss Chastain. Ozzy mentioned you'd be stopping by for an interview."

"Yes, I'm speaking with all our potential buyers. Well. Of course, he *is* still on the potential list."

So why did she make it sound as if he was not? Lennon would not intrude on the complexities of their business deal. "I'm sorry but he's in his office until noon. I'm sure, though, he'd want me to let him know you are here."

"Why don't you hold off on that. Let him work. It'll give us a chance to talk. Would that be all right with you?"

"Of course." But what was there to talk about? What to do? She had hours to entertain this woman. And the idea of saying something wrong loomed over one shoulder.

Don't panic! You've got this.

"Uh, I was actually just going for a walk along the beach."

"That sounds delicious. I've been bouncing from flight to flight all morning. Is there somewhere I can freshen up? I've brought along different shoes as well. One never visits a villa on the beach without preparing."

"Absolutely. Come this way."

Lennon showed her to the bathroom off the beach room in the back of the house, and while she waited for her to come out she texted Ozzy.

He didn't reply. Must be super busy.

With a set of her shoulders, Lennon decided she could help him out. It was what he'd asked her to do anyway. Now to make Cozy Closets believe Ozzy Wilder was a solid, stable man with aspirations toward family.

CHAPTER NINE

THE WALK ALONG the beach started with light banter about how fabulous Greece was and how Miss Chastain wanted to visit a few islands before heading back home to New York. She'd brought along sandals and every so often would stretch out her arms and tilt back her head, declaring she needed to take a real vacation and soon.

"You must be very busy," Lennon said. "You're CEO?"

"Yes, I've been at the helm since my mother stepped down a decade ago. She was the one who started the business."

"Oh, yes, with Ozzy's grandmother, Eliza."

Amaris made a disagreeing noise. Ozzy had not filled her in on the argument between the original founders, but he had made it clear Cozy Closets had been as good as stolen from Eliza, that she had been literally forced out of her own company. Lennon didn't want to delve too deeply into that with Miss Chastain. It could make the deal even more difficult for Ozzy.

"So," she added brightly, "why are you selling now?"

"It's the vacation thing," Amaris said. "The wind and sea are calling my name. And I'm at a place where I can afford to retire. And why not do it when I'm still young enough to enjoy it?"

"Smart. But if you don't mind me asking, then why *not* sell to Ozzy? If you're so eager to get started on your next chapter?"

"Well, there's the board to please. And even when Cozy leaves my hands, it will always mean something to me. I side with the board's concerns that Mr. Wilder will take Cozy in the wrong direction."

They neared the stone steps leading up the side of the beach to a grassy hill, and Lennon paused to turn directly to Amaris. "Please, you shouldn't be concerned. I know Wilder's Wardrobes has a certain brand for masculine and clean design, but that's just a brand. It's not who Ozzy is."

"There's not a thing wrong with those closets," Amaris said. "It's just not us. Cozy's image is wholesome. Cozycore. And even if Mr. Wilder did leave Cozy as is at first, I'm not sure it would remain so. Can he be trusted?"

Lennon swallowed. *She* wanted to trust him.

"You are aware the history of Cozy Closets

and how it relates to your boyfriend?" Amaris added.

That must be the bad blood with Eliza. How much to reveal without exposing something Ozzy didn't want her to?

"About its founders?" Lennon said carefully.

"Eliza Wilder was the founder alongside my mother Sandra Chastain. When Eliza walked away, Mom was left with it all. Legally. Including some very important patents. I fear Mr. Wilder may only be after us for those."

"Oh." Eliza hadn't *walked away.* Not according to Ozzy. But different perspectives? Arguing with Amaris wasn't going to endear Ozzy to the company.

"You know, he's aware of all that. And...certainly Cozy Closets brings immense value to Wilder's Wardrobes. But it's more that Ozzy is ready for a change. As you are. Or rather, he wants to expand and show the world that he is more than just one thing."

"Sexy?" Amaris said with disdain.

"You have to admit, that was a great marketing campaign. But that's all it was. And sure, Ozzy is a heck of a sexy man, but that's all exterior. He's got depth. A heart. He really is all about family. I know he'd do well by your brand."

"He doesn't even know our brand."

"He does. At least, he's mentioned many of the

styles to me." Thankful for having done some research, she did her best. "For example, your Summer Dreams line. The one focused on teenage girls. I love those closets! They are functional and frilly at the same time. But also, they give girls a proud sense of their own style and space."

Amaris looked open to hearing more.

"If I would have had such a space when I was younger, I might have spent all my time in it!" Lennon declared. "I would have invited in all my friends for a party. Your closets are so personal, and suited to the age groups yet they grow with those younger kids to adulthood. And the Adventurer line is amazing. Growing from baseballs and dinosaurs to archaeology and fine leathers? That's Ozzy's favorite." Fingers crossed.

"You know a lot about Cozy Closets, Miss Hart. I'm impressed."

"I'm not trying to impress you. Well, yes, I am. I mean, you did come here to investigate Ozzy's personal life, which includes me. You have to know he isn't the bad boy that ad campaign made him out to be. Maybe he once used to be a little wild, but now he's just so..." Dreamy. "...settled. Ready for a family."

"Is that so? So the two of you...?"

"Oh. I mean, we're serious, but we've only been dating a few months."

"Oh? Mr. Wilder mentioned something about the two of you being high school sweethearts?"

"Uh, yes. We did date in high school." Oh, Ozzy, really? The man really had panicked. "I just want you to know that Ozzy understands more than you think he does. He's a genius when it comes to closets. He's going to preserve the quality and uniqueness of your designs, I'm sure."

"You're sure? Is that just a guess, Miss Hart?"

"I'm very sure." Lennon spied someone walking down the beach in a bright purple caftan. Eliza. Not the person she wanted Amaris to meet right now. "We should head inside. We can talk over a glass of guava lemonade the chef brewed up this morning. It has a touch of mint in it. It's amazing."

Taking the lead, she stepped up the rocks and Amaris followed. It was a little hazardous with loose stones and sand cluttered in the grass edging the rise, Lennon noted, and she was surprised Ozzy hadn't installed a railing. Weren't these stone steps frequently used?

She glanced back to find Amaris took the steps carefully. When she reached the top of the hill, she waited and Amaris reached out. Lennon caught her hand and hoisted her up to the hilltop.

Amaris chuckled and said, "I'm a little out of shape. But look at me. Ready to begin that next adventurous chapter." She lifted her arms in a triumphant pump and— "Oh!"

It was that excited step backward that would result in a trying few days for Lennon and Ozzy.

CHAPTER TEN

"MR. WILDER, I'm quite embarrassed at all the trouble I've caused," Amaris Chastain said after Ozzy had shaken her hand.

She sat on a sofa in the last available guest bedroom. She'd tripped at the top of the stone stairs that he really needed to mark as unsafe if he were to do more entertaining. Lennon had called him as he was walking out of the office, and he'd had a doctor here within the hour to look her over. Sprained ankle. A severe tear to the ligament. She was unable to put weight on it or walk. The doctor recommended she absolutely stay off her feet for the next forty-eight hours, and then he'd reassess if she would need crutches or extended care. He'd left her with the name of a physical therapist in New York for when she returned home.

"It's not a problem, Miss Chastain. I'm sorry, those steps should have been marked as being unsafe. It's not an area that gets regular use. You'll stay here while you rest your ankle?"

"Oh, I couldn't possibly. I have a hotel room in town. And your girlfriend told me about the wedding this weekend. I'd just be in the way."

"Nonsense."

Where was Lemon? He didn't have a chance to speak to her and learn what she and Chastain had talked about. Also, he'd left Lemon to handle his guest on her own. He appreciated her taking the initiative but felt awful that she'd had to do so. And because he'd been embroiled in his work, a guest had been injured on his property. She could sue. If he didn't treat her with kid gloves, this ruse could go horribly wrong. Not the way to win Cozy Closets.

On the other hand, if she were to be here a few days, he may have more time to win her over.

"This room wasn't taken by any of the guests. I insist you stay at least the forty-eight hours the doctor recommended you keep your foot elevated. You're beachside so you'll have an excellent view. And you'll be waited on. Anything you need you only have to ask."

"Oh. Well." She sighed and looked out the patio doors. The blue waters glistened. A view that always made him grateful. "There isn't a view from my hotel room."

"Did you and Lemon have a good chat?"

"Lemon?"

He rubbed his jaw. "It's my nickname for her. I've called her that since we were kids."

"High school sweethearts. So precious. Miss Hart is lovely. And she knows so much about Cozy Closets."

Was that so? When had Lemon done research on Cozy Closets?

"I guess I haven't much choice but to settle in and get some remote work done," Chastain said. "And we did have an interview scheduled. If you insist I stay?"

As long as Eliza didn't find out they had the CEO of Cozy Closets staying here, they should be fine. Ozzy couldn't imagine his grandma having a blazing argument with anyone, but he didn't know how deep her anger went over having been ousted from the company.

And his conversation with Lemon when she had suggested he keep Cozy Closets as is had given him pause.

"Yes, that interview," he said. "I have an idea or two about how Wilder's Wardrobes can smoothly incorporate Cozy with minimal changes. If you're feeling up to it later, perhaps we can discuss that. I want to show you that I will handle Cozy Closets respectfully should you allow my bid to stand against the others you're considering."

"Well." Amaris wriggled her nose. Not exactly in disgust, but she wasn't going to make this easy for him. "I am tired from the travel and now… this." She gestured to her ankle. "Perhaps later. Or even tomorrow. We'll see how I'm feeling."

"Of course," he said. "I'll send in the housekeeper to make sure you have everything you need, along with some lunch. I have to rush out because there are some deliveries arriving soon. Wedding stuff. But I'm sure Lemon will stop in to check on you. She's…caring like that."

It felt odd to say. He didn't know that about her. But it was obvious in her smile and her easy manner around him. And the fact that she'd spoken so highly of him to Chastain.

"Do bring my bag to me. I've my laptop in there," Chastain said. "Then I'll be good to go. I'm still not completely sold on you, Mr. Wilder."

Ozzy set the bag beside the sofa within reach. "We've had a bad start." He glanced down to her ankle, wrapped in a compression bandage. A bag of ice sat on top. "But you'll see that I am the best one to acquire Cozy Closets."

"Yes, well…we'll see." She dug out the laptop and gestured he leave.

Ozzy closed the bedroom door behind him just as Eliza walked by.

"Has another guest arrived?" she asked as he put his hand on her shoulder to lead her toward the main rooms.

"Yes, but she's not feeling well. Might have

the flu. A friend of…mine, actually. From work. We're going to keep her comfy and see if she feels like joining us in a day or so."

"Oh, that's terrible. Maybe I should look in on her? Give her some comfort."

"No, Grandma, I don't want you going in there. You might catch whatever it is she may have."

"Pft! I'm healthy as an ox."

He lured her away from the one door he hoped she never touched. "How healthy are oxen, really?"

Lemon was wearing the moomoo again today. It did little to accentuate her figure the way the red dress had, but Ozzy had to smile at the way she worked it. He caught her unawares in the vast living area where the one wall was entirely windows looking over the sea.

With phone in hand, probably taking a selfie, she strolled with her arms out and head grandly tilted back. As if a majestic queen overseeing her—furniture. The lemon diamond glinted. Every time he looked at her she commanded his attention. She had it all. Beauty, grace, talent, and that she was unaware of her good qualities was sexy in its own way. Lemon didn't have to do a thing to catch his eye beyond existing.

She suddenly swayed and spun, twirling as if receiving praise from an invisible audience.

Glamour girl. Yet when she saw him she stumbled against the corner of a sofa and fell backward onto the plush cushions.

"How long have you been standing there?"

"Just long enough to..." Want her. "Uh, you're so..." *Say it!*

No, it didn't feel possible to be so direct with her. To even insinuate they might consider this fake dating as something a little more real.

Ozzy wandered inside and plopped onto the sofa beside her, which sent her lightweight body toppling toward the edge. He had to grab her shoulder so she wouldn't fly onto the carpet.

"Talk about a wild ride." Lemon tugged at the moomoo and then turned and pulled up a leg. A tap to her cell phone turned the screen dark. "Just felt like a selfie moment. Not every day a girl wears such elegant fabric. This thing *is* silk."

"It's hideous."

"But it's silk?"

"Are you asking me or telling me?"

"I've never owned silk before. And it did cost you a lot so I should get my money's worth out of it."

"*My* money's worth. And consider that debt paid. Toss that thing. Or rather, donate it to a seniors' home." He mocked a shudder.

She shoved his shoulder playfully. "It's not that bad."

"You did notice Grandma is wearing virtually the same one?"

"Sure but… Do you think it makes me look like a dork?"

"It's not your style, Lemon." Or anyone's, in truth. But still, he'd seen beyond the ugly fabric to the beautiful woman beneath. "Besides, you could never be a dork."

"Oh, come on, I am the dork queen. I used to walk the high school halls with braces, glasses *and* I sported a violin case."

Ozzy laughed. True. "You want to talk dork-atude? Lemon, I own a closet empire. *Closets.* With shelves. And shoeboxes. And tie hooks. It doesn't get any dorkier than that."

"Ozzy, your closets are just plain sexy. Not a whisper of dork to them."

Her encouragement sunk through his skin like warm sunshine. It felt different from a comradely pat on the back from a coworker or a loving hug from his grandmother. Lemon's validation tapped at that little boy's closed heart of his, and said "I care about you."

"A lot of design and marketing went into making them sexy," he said, "but when all is said and done, I'm putting shelves in people's rooms so they can store their clothes. It's not likc I'm selling Lamborghinis or smartwatches."

"We all have clothes. We all need someplace to

store them. But I won't fight for the dork crown. It's yours," she announced sweetly. "So did you look in on Amaris?"

What he'd thought would be a quick visit, answer a few questions, look happily in love, had turned into a disaster. Add to that, having to continue this charade? The line between acting and feeling was growing thinner. And he wasn't sure how to act now.

That was the thing: *Was* he acting? More and more his attraction to Lemon kept sidetracking him from putting on a ruse. His reactions to her were real, not forced.

A glance to Lemon always landed on her freckles. From there he couldn't resist swimming in her gaze awhile, feeling as though he'd won some sort of fake girlfriend lottery. That she had dived into the act showed her generosity. And every tilt of her head, or wriggle of her mouth into a questioning moue revealed her sensual appeal.

"Yes, Amaris is going to be here a couple of days while the swelling goes down in her ankle," he said. "And… I remembered what you said about keeping the Cozy Closets brand as is so I punted again and told her I'd like to discuss how we plan to incorporate her company into mine without changing it."

"Yeah? I'm so glad!" She tilted her head at him. "Wait. Another lie?"

Ozzy sighed. This was getting deeper than he'd ever thought it could get.

"Don't tell me you panicked again," she said. "You are not the panicking sort. So that must mean you have altered your plans to ditch the company after you've won the bid?"

"It's a possibility. It's still going to be up to Grandma. But I've got to come up with some good ideas to pitch to Chastain."

"I can help. I know all about Cozy now. I did research."

"I heard about that. Amaris was impressed. You didn't have to do that, Lemon."

"I'm pretty sure your girlfriend would have an interest in your company and your business goals. Besides, I like doing research on just about anything."

He placed his curved fingers above her head and lightly set them on her hair. "Dork crown is all yours again."

"And just so you know? The Cozy Closets Adventurer line is your favorite."

"Noted. All right, Miss Know-It-All, let's brainstorm."

"Hey, kids!" Eliza called from the kitchen as she wandered through with a cup of coffee and walked right on by toward the pantry.

"We can't let Amaris know the one woman she holds a grudge against is actually here," Lemon said. "You know, I have a suspicion the reason she doesn't want to sell to you isn't so much you as it is that old feud between her mother and Eliza."

"You think?" He'd seriously considered that. But it had been decades. Was Amaris using the lacking family values angle as a means to cover her true feelings about the rift between Eliza and Sandra? "We need to keep Grandma occupied and away from that guest room wing."

"Eliza begins baking today. She'll be busy. My parents are arriving this evening. And I'm freaking out! I just saw Mom five days ago. She'll never believe I started dating you so quickly without telling her. I'm always filling her in on my pitiful romantic life."

"It hits me right here—" Ozzy thumped his chest "—to hear you say your romance has been pitiful. What's up with that?"

She pointed to herself. "Dork."

"Dorks find love all the time."

"Yeah, well..." Lemon sighed. "Promise that you haven't forgotten about fixing me up?"

"I haven't. There's a friend of mine on the island, Dimitri. He's a prompt engineer. That's about as dorky as it gets."

"What's a prompt engineer?"

"Something to do with telling AI exactly what to do to get a desired result. Big name companies hire him for megabucks."

"Is he sexy?"

Ozzy shrugged a helpless gesture.

"Right. Not a good judge of your friends' sex appeal. But I trust you to vet a good match for me."

"Will do. But you're going to have to play up the fake around your parents since Amaris is now here for a couple of days. Just stick to the plan—we finally realized we were interested in one another and…we gave into it."

Yeah. That wasn't a lie at all.

"Hmm, I suppose I could have been waiting to spring my new romance on Mom when she gets here. It doesn't jive with the timeline we gave your grandma though."

"Don't mention timelines. This will all be over in a few days, Lemon. Promise."

"Yeah, okay."

She sounded about enthusiastic for their fictional breakup as he did. Because what if it could become nonfiction? Not a moment had passed since Lemon had walked through his front door that he hadn't wondered over that long-ago curiosity for her. The subtle attraction. And the not-so-subtle real attraction he was experiencing now.

"Hey guys!" A couple of bridesmaids walked in. "There you are. We need your help at the dais. The wedding planner isn't due until tomorrow and the DJ, who drove in for a few hours, wants to get his music synched for the ceremony. And since Harry went to town to buy a gift for Claire, we need stand-ins for the bride and groom. Come on!" One of the women gestured for them to follow her. "This'll be great practice for if you two ever get hitched!"

Lemon gave Ozzy a look that was half worried but also half excited. He could see it in her eyes. She was enjoying every moment of this fake.

"Ready to say 'I do'?" she asked.

"Let's do it." He held out his hand and Lemon took it. With a tug, he lifted her from the couch in a leap and she landed with a bouncing step. Like tossing around a fairy.

Yeah, she was fun. And he didn't mind them sharing the dork crown. But now that he'd mentioned Dimitri, that would mean he'd have to actually contact him and see if he was interested in taking Lemon out on a date. The guy would do it as a favor to Ozzy.

Just as he had done a favor to Harry by taking his sister to the prom? That hadn't ended well at all. But at least Ozzy could claim he'd tried, right?

Lemon wanted a romance and to fall in love?

Same, Lemon. Same.

CHAPTER ELEVEN

THE DJ HAD put together a playlist for the ceremony. Claire had requested all Taylor Swift songs, and she wanted them timed perfectly to the big moments.

As directed by one of the bridesmaids, Lennon stood beside Ozzy at the end of the aisle. Even with empty chairs and no flowers the mood was bubbly and fun, as if the ceremony were happening today. The hope of someday walking down the aisle herself bounced her on her feet. So when she took Ozzy's hand and flashed a side-look at him, she had to remind herself that this, too, was a fake.

"Do you want to get married someday?" she asked him.

"Sure," he said out the side of his mouth. They both faced front, their attention on what the DJ was doing. "I'm all about family. Remember?"

"I mean for real. Dork."

Something about his smile reassured her. Nothing fake about it. "Yes, for real, Lemon. But

I'm afraid I didn't have a good example of how to parent and I don't think I'd be any good at it myself. There was the babysitting stint, so I've had *some* experience. But don't ask about that."

Don't ask? How could she *not* after a mysterious drop like that? Babysitting? Ozzy? No way. But besides that curious morsel, his parents were the worst. She hated them for that.

"I'm curious about the babysitting but will respect your request." Compelled, she lifted his hand and gave it a kiss. "You'll do just fine when the day comes that you become a father."

"Thanks, Lemon." He squeezed her hand. "What about you?"

"I also have a curiosity about doing the family thing. More than that. I do want to make a family."

"No manifesting a family?"

"I keep my manifestations much lighter. The big stuff is entirely out of our hands."

"A hot summer romance isn't a big thing?"

"Sure it is, but it's not do-or-die." It had felt that way when she'd put up her reel a few days ago. Wasn't it her turn to experience heart-pounding, stomach-fluttering romance? To finally overcome her fear of being let down, of being dumped or refused? To take that next step toward love? "I mean, it's just for my vacation. Just something to get my confidence up. Not like I'm hoping for happily-ever-after."

He eyed her suspiciously. Yeah, she didn't believe that lie either.

"Okay, people!" The DJ clapped, drawing everyone's attention to the front. "Claire has some specific moments she wants highlighted with music during the ceremony, so we need to walk through the whole thing and I'll being timing it out. Is that my fake bride and groom at the back?"

Ozzy raised his hand. "Here."

Lennon nudged his elbow. "Here? We're not in school."

"Feels like it," he muttered to her.

As the music began, the DJ motioned for each of the players to walk on their cue. Lennon paid close attention. After all, this was an assignment, and she liked to do things right. Yeah, so she wore the dork crown proudly.

Beside her Ozzy checked his phone. She nudged him. "Ozzy!"

"Sorry. Work messages. Right, I'm the groom. Gotta look sharp."

She rolled her eyes and he leaned in and whispered, "One day they'll roll right out of your head."

Stifling a giggle, she shook her head. "You sound like someone's grandma."

"Guilty." He tucked away his phone and glanced down at her. That grin was enough to—damn, the man was too sexy for a woman who had opened herself to welcoming romance. And hot romance, at that. "What? Have I grown horns?"

Shoot. Had she just been ogling the man? *Get your act, together, Lennon!*

At that moment the music stopped. The entire wedding party, save the best man, was up front, angled off from the center. The DJ called, "We need the groom up front!"

"That's you, honeybun."

"See you in a few." Ozzy strolled down the aisle, giving a grand bow to much applause as he arrived on the dais.

"Of course, the groom will already be up here, along with his best man," the DJ corrected. "My bad. Now, do we have the flower girl and boy?"

"Not until tomorrow," one of the bridesmaids said.

"Then we'll have two of you stand in. I need to mark time cues."

They went through fake flower sprinkling, and one of the groomsmen cradled a beer can as if a pillow with a ring. Then the bridal march, which no woman would ever mistake, began.

Lennon lifted her chin, clasped her hands before her as if holding a bouquet, and eyed the DJ. He held up one finger to stay her. And then…

The moment turned surreal in a snap. She was about to walk down the aisle to stand beside the one guy. *That* guy. The one who had owned her heart so many years ago. Having a summer romance with Ozzy had never occurred to her when she'd been flying across the ocean a few days ago. Was she too far out in left field to consider they might work now, all these years later? Because, yes, she was seeing him in a new light. And that light shone on him brightly.

Time to manifest—whatever the universe thought was best for her.

With a nod from the DJ, Lennon began a slow, measured walk down the aisle. As she did, she nodded to the imaginary family members sitting to either side of the aisle. Walking toward the sexiest man alive. And he—actually, Ozzy *beamed* at her as she approached. She'd never seen him smile so effortlessly. With a megadose of sexy. That smile did something to her heart. Made her stop believing she was a nerdy violin player who tried to manifest things as a replacement for self-esteem. And that maybe she could trust him never to break her heart again.

She floated the last few steps to the dais, exuding a new confidence.

Lennon stepped up beside Ozzy, and he took her hand. It was…a moment.

That was quickly obliterated by the DJ's voice

and a cut in the music. "All right, boys and girls. Next the pastor does his spiel. Then…"

Ozzy's long fingers wrapped around hers and he squeezed. Was it possible to see her future in a man's eyes? If that future held starlight in the midnight sky, it was. His hand was so warm, the clasp firm and yet gentle. He had her. Would never let go.

Did this moment have to end?

"Now the bride and groom have a candle lighting moment, so we cue more music…"

A gentle love song filled the air. And even though they had nothing to do, Lennon felt as if they were doing everything. A montage of what her life with Ozzy could be like flashed through her brain. A breezy—but hot—summer romance. Lennon never leaving Greece. Quitting her job at the flower shop to be with her man. Ozzy asking her to marry him. The vows. The honeymoon. The baby carriage.

Holy carp. It was happening. She was falling for him all over again.

She'd promised herself she wouldn't allow that to happen again.

"And now," the DJ said again, "the couple are pronounced happily married. The cue to kiss brings on more music."

A Taylor Swift love song played and suddenly Lennon found herself leaning in toward Ozzy.

Seeking. Following her pining heart. She stood at the curb…

From behind her someone called, "Kiss!"

And then another person said, "Kiss!"

Ozzy leaned closer. Nothing between them but three inches of air… The music rose dramatically. Someone clapped even as the voices flanking them faded into a blur. Lennon's heart thundered.

This was it! Forget about all those reservations. She wanted this kiss. She was *owed* this kiss.

Ozzy thrust up his hand between their almost-kissing lips. "Sorry," he muttered.

"Oh." Lennon straightened. Shook her head.

It had almost happened! The kiss she'd always wanted. But an inch from reality. It would have fit perfectly in their ploy to play a couple. What happily in love couple did not kiss? And yet, Ozzy had stopped it.

Someone behind her muttered, "Really?"

"Right!" Lennon burst out. Her ability to roll with the punches kicking in. "Wouldn't want to spoil the real thing."

"Exactly," Ozzy said, joining the ruse. "The only time I want to kiss my beautiful girlfriend at the altar is when we say our vows. It's gotta be perfect."

"Saving ourselves!" Lennon nodded effusively and looked around for agreement from the wedding party, who eventually nodded and agreed.

Ozzy gave her a weak shrug. She patted him on the shoulder. “Good call.”

“We did have a rule,” he muttered.

Right. How quickly she had forgotten.

The DJ announced, “Let’s begin the exit! The happily married couple go first!”

As the music escorted them down the aisle, Ozzy took Lennon’s hand. But this time his grip didn’t feel as secure and confidant. “Sorry about that,” he said. “I panicked.”

So maybe he did have a panic mode. It seemed to be working overtime at the moment.

“Don’t worry. No need to kiss me to make it look good.”

But still. Just a little peck might have been more convincing than none at all. But there it was: He hadn’t wanted to kiss her. Again.

When they reached the end of the aisle, Lennon tugged her hand from his. “I’m going to… check on Amaris. See ya!”

Quickly, she made her way down the beach so no one could see her struggle with the confusing mix of emotions storming her brain.

That almost-kiss had felt so much like prom night part two. Then, she’d stood at the curb after prom waiting as Ozzy had silently gazed at her. His eyes had been wide and seeking, yet soft and so intense. He’d smelled like fruit punch and chocolate cupcakes. She’d thought he would kiss her. It had felt like a certainty. So, she'd blurted out, "Did you really mean it when you said I was your girl?"

He'd whispered "my girl" in her ear as they'd slow-danced beneath the giant disco ball. The moment so perfect, she'd clutched him tighter and fallen away from reality. It was real. He liked her as much as she liked him.

Until the curb.

Ozzy had bitten his lip and shaken his head. "I'm so sorry, Lemon, I shouldn't have said that. It was a stupid slip. It's… I know you could never fall in love with me. My parents taught me that much. And there's your brother. It would be weird to date my best friend's sister. I do like you but… This is how it's gotta be. We can't date. Ever."

As if on cue, a car filled with his friends had pulled up and had asked him to join them for a keg party. With a glance to her—he hadn't asked her to join him—and a reluctant nod from her, he'd then said "See ya, Lemon!" and had jumped in the back of the convertible.

Lennon had watched the car drive away. The smell of oil in the breezy spring air still so fresh in her memory. Her heart shattering. The previous two hours of dancing and partying inside the gymnasium had meant nothing. She wasn't his girl.

And now.

Once landing on the beach, Lennon paused before the beach house and turned to look up at the wedding party, who lingered around the dais. The DJ blasted dance tunes. She'd wanted that kiss at the altar. Like a fool who had never learned her lesson.

But *why* had she wanted a kiss? Was she *still* crushing on the guy all these years later? Surely her heart had grown up and matured and…shoot. There were still threads of adoration and desire running through her veins. All for Ozzy. He'd become such an amazing man. A professional success. Smart. Kind. Sexy. Still a little damaged by his past. And still woven through with remnants of that teenage boy she had so adored.

And the thing that had hurt her worst? Much as he'd made it sound as though he'd wanted to date her, he didn't think she could ever love him because his parents had taught him he was unlovable. So he'd walked away from her. That rejection had torn apart her teenage heart.

She did know him differently now. Understood the reason behind his fleeing from a situation where he thought he might get rejected once again. Was she being too hard on Ozzy by expecting him to meet her foolish desires without allowing him room for his issues?

From inside the villa, she spied movement. Amaris waved and beckoned to her. The woman had to be going stir-crazy in her exile to a single room. Lennon started toward the house. She stole one last glance at the dais then spied Ozzy looking down at her. She waved. He waved back.

The man had reached in and touched her heart. Again. And at a time when she'd thought to be over him, she wanted to sneak up closer, like a curious cat, weave around his space to see if he would either nudge her away or maybe, just maybe, pull her close for that long-awaited kiss.

CHAPTER TWELVE

OZZY'S GRANDMA SAT before the kitchen counter making fondant flowers. Yes, he knew the term for that flattened, sweet colored powdered sugar and water mixture that she used to carve out designs for cakes. When younger, he'd sat at the end of the counter many times observing her alchemy. She'd always let him eat the discards.

He found his place at the end of the counter and caught his chin in his hand. Eliza continued to work so he watched quietly. It was nice having her here. He wondered if he should extend an invitation for her to stay in the bungalow through the summer. She had no family back in Minnesota. She might even enjoy Paris if he could find a place for her. She wasn't getting any younger, and he didn't ever want to see her in a nursing home.

"How did the rehearsal go?" she asked, drawing her cutting tool along the smooth pink fondant.

"The DJ got his cues set."

Eliza nodded. Worked for a while. Ozzy was content to watch her. This simple quiet was a treasure. Life had gotten busy. The Paris office was small, but the warehouse was always bustling. He enjoyed being in the midst of the carpentry and design side of the business. Of overseeing and delegating. Of being in control. Which was why he'd agreed to host the wedding.

But this moment sitting at the counter with his grandma?

"Nice," he said.

"It is," she agreed. "I watched a little of the rehearsal. Why didn't you kiss her?"

"Huh?"

His grandmother looked up at him, blue eyes gentle yet delving. He knew exactly what she meant. And she knew he knew. She bowed over her work again.

He wanted to tell her the truth. It wasn't fair to lie to her like this.

"Lemon thought we should keep what happened on the altar special," he said carefully. "Save it for our wedding day. I mean, if we ever have one. You know. We've only been dating a short time."

"Mmm-hmm," his grandmother uttered. Not believing?

He didn't much believe that himself. He'd told Lemon he wanted to do the family thing someday, and he'd meant it. But really, who was he to think he could convince Amaris Chastain that he was a family man? It had been just Ozzy and his grandma for a long time. He had no example of what family was beyond the pseudo-family of the Harts.

He held the Hart family in high esteem. Mr. and Mrs. Hart treated him as a son. There wasn't a holiday he wasn't invited to visit. And if he were in the States, he always stopped in to say hi. The emotional high he got from being in their presence went a long way in burying the ache of his parents' betrayal. An ache that drilled deep, never completely erased. What Lemon had said about him believing what he told himself about being unlovable was true. But he'd told himself that for so long, how to change the script?

"The Harts arrive later this evening," he said. Because a subject change was needed. "I've put them in the room across from yours."

"It's been a while since I've seen them. I look forward to catching up. Hand me that crimper, will you?"

He reached for the device that looked like a mini pizza cutter; it would ruffle the edges of a flower. Yes, he knew the tools of the trade. She'd taught him a lot. Including giving him the impetus to start his own closet design company. "Grandma?"

"Yes, Oscar, is there something you need to tell me?"

She knew. She had to. But he wasn't prepared to confess, especially with Chastain staying in the house and—there was too much bad blood between Eliza and the Chastains. Best to get through the wedding and worry about the truth afterward.

"I was thinking that maybe you'd like to stay here through the summer."

Eliza set down her tools and looked up at him, blowing at a strand of hair that had fallen from her clips. "I would like that. But would I be in your way? You know, between you and Lennon?"

"Not at all. Lemon is…"

Expecting to dive into a romance with anyone but him following the wedding. Intending to walk away from their fake. But the idea of watching Lemon go on a date with someone else…? A different kind of ache stirred within Ozzy's chest, and it wasn't anything at all like parental betrayal. Would he be jealous if she went on a date with Dimitri? Hell, yes.

"Lemon and I are still long distance. For now. But you don't need to worry about the living situation. Lemon adores you. I would love to have you stay. The bungalow could be yours for however long you wish to stay."

"You're a dear, Oscar. I don't have much to

return to back home. Save a few friends. Our book club went bust last year, and the library isn't taking volunteers anymore. I have so much time on my hands and nothing to do beyond a little gardening."

"There's a lot for you to do on the island. Beachcombing. Shopping. You could go hiking with me."

"I've still got some gumption, Oscar. You think I won't take you up on that?"

"I hope you do."

"Then, yes, I'd love to stay. Just until you head back to Paris."

"We can talk about the possibility of you in Paris later this fall." He swung around the counter and gave her a hug. "I love you, Grandma. It'll be good to have you here. Now I'm going to find Lemon. I want to make sure her parents' room is to their liking before they get here."

He walked off but Eliza called after him, "She's good for you, Oscar!"

Ozzy waved but didn't reply. Lemon was… well, yes, he liked having her around. And that almost-kiss had been something, hadn't it? He could have kissed her. Easily. He wanted to kiss her, to know the shape of her lips against his. To be so comfortable with a person that a kiss felt unavoidable.

But would it be a lie, too? He didn't want to

hurt Lemon again. He knew how it felt to pine for something and to deny it. He was losing track of what was real, and what was fake.

The script in his heart needed a rewrite. Dare he reach for love?

A lilting violin melody lured Ozzy into his bedroom. Lemon stood on the far side before the window, her back to him, her body swaying to what he recognized as a classical piece.

Creeping toward the bed, he glided onto it and lay on his back, hands behind his head, and closed his eyes. He loved all types of music, including classical. Mozart was great to play when he was on a deadline and needed to crunch numbers for a project.

The last time Ozzy had taken a moment to close his eyes and sink into music was… He couldn't recall. In high school he'd been a big heavy metal fan. He and Harry had once driven all the way to the Twin Cities to see a Metallica concert. Epic.

Lost in the music, Lemon swayed. Still hadn't noticed he was in the room. She was so talented. Surprisingly, she had never sought to create a career utilizing her skill. As part of a symphony orchestra. Or even solo touring. Her body became the music as she shifted and tilted her head, drawing out her bowing arm and creating gorgeous tones. She wore a gossamer white beach cover-up over a bikini. The sun shining through the windows made the cover-up look like a floaty sheen, revealing her straight lines with very little curves. The dancing and the music and the shimmery fabric all coalesced into a sexy image. Like a fairy playing an enchanted song. Luring him closer, drawing a smile onto his mouth and a teasing want through his veins.

He *wanted* Lemon. In his arms. At his mouth. On this bed. And the thought did not so much startle him as confirm what he'd always known.

"Oh!" The music crashed to a halt.

Ozzy leaned up onto his elbows and winked at her.

"How long have you been lying there?"

"Five minutes?" he said.

Lennon dropped her bowing arm; the violin remained tucked between chin and collarbone. While bowing an arpeggio she'd spun and spied Ozzy sprawled on the bed. Eyes closed. Wiggling a leg, tapping a foot. Listening to her?

How embarrassing!

"Don't stop. I like listening to you play, Lemon."

"I don't give private concerts." She stepped down from before the window and set her violin in the open case. "You scared the carp out of me."

"Don't you mean crap?"

"I don't like that word. It's squicky."

"Squicky is a word that feels squicky to me. So what was the name of that song? I like it."

"The 'Brandenburg Concerto No. 2' by Bach. I just got a text from Claire asking me if, in addition to playing at the dance, I could play them out after they say their vows."

"No Swift? Wow. Did you check with the DJ? That guy has everything timed to the millisecond."

"I'm going to text him. It was a surprise that Claire asked me to do it. Not sure Bach mixes well with Taylor Swift. But it's much better than the Paganini I initially suggested. My favorite composer."

"If you don't give private concerts, then why agree to a wedding concert?"

"Private meaning one-on-one. I can perform for a small gathering. It's been a part of my self-confidence journey. And I've only got that one final step remaining."

"Which step is that?"

"The one where I allow myself to fall in love." And enough talk about that with *him*. "What are you doing in here anyway? I mean, sorry. It *is* your room."

She sat on the edge of the bed and lay back, so

her head was even with his, their bodies and legs going out on opposite sides of the bed.

"I was heading down to check on Amaris when I heard the delicious tones of a maestro and was lured in here."

With a giggle Lennon slapped her hand out, and it landed on her phone, which she'd tossed after reading the comments on some of her posts. "Never a maestro, that's for sure."

"Why not? Why didn't you pursue a musical career?"

"I'm not *that* talented. I mean, I'll acccpt that I have some skill. But I'm no Lindsey Stirling. Or David Garrett, for that matter. Do you know he mixes in AC/DC with Bach and Paganini?"

"Sounds like my kind of entertainer. We should catch a concert some time."

"That would be cool. He's from Germany but tours the world. Should I check when his next concert is?"

"Go for it. So instead of playing in some famous symphony orchestra you chose influencing?"

"I don't know that I influence too many people. But I've never been a nine-to-fiver." Lennon scrolled through the violinist's site. Not currently on tour. There went her opportunity to spend more time with Ozzy. The agony! "The fact that people can actually make a living posting on Tik-

Tok and putting up their thoughts on life is a boon for me."

"What are the dreams you want to manifest for yourself?"

"Deep stuff, Ozzy."

"I thought you said we needed to learn more about each other?"

"I don't think Miss Chastain is going to dig too deeply on our knowledge of one another. I chatted with her after the rehearsal and she was telling me about her plans for travel. I think I've kind of sold her on me."

"You did. Thank you for that. But that still doesn't mean I can't be interested in your dreams. Talk to me."

She turned her head to look at him. Upside-down, his smile was still charming. They should take advantage of this quiet moment. Because the next few days would be a whirlwind, and too soon this easy connection they'd developed would be severed. Hot summer romance? Meh. If that romance never manifested? She wouldn't be as upset as she should be. Because she'd gotten something better in the time she was spending with Ozzy.

Of course, a kiss at the altar would have been the cherry on top.

Let it go, Lennon.

"My dreams are what most want," she said.

"Shelter, community, a job that makes me happy, and…the freedom to explore the world."

"Tell me more about this exploring."

"I don't know. I like to learn new things. After talking to Amaris, I realized traveling would be fun."

"Where would you go if you had the cash?"

"Arizona."

"Arizona?" He sounded surprised.

"I think it would be cool to hike in the Joshua Tree Forest. See insects I've never seen before. Take photos of all the cacti and cool rocks. There's rarely a time when I'm hiking that I don't come home with a rock in my pocket. What about you?"

He turned to lie on his side, so Lennon rolled onto her side, too. The man's eyes were a golden glinting brown. Better than chocolate cake. If she could have ever imagined Ozzy living this lifestyle, looking like this, and them playacting at a couple she would have thought she'd lost her mind.

"Do you know," he said, "I have the money and freedom to do things like explore but I don't."

"Why not? You don't need to work. You could travel the world and see all the things."

"Like a David Garrett concert?"

"I checked. He's not on tour. Major bummer. Come on, you have the cash. You should be out there learning new things, eating new foods, climbing mountains or whatever you want."

"All of the above sounds great, but I don't have anyone to see the things with. Life should be lived…with someone who makes you feel…" He sighed and shook his head. "I don't want to do that stuff alone, Lemon."

Same thing she'd been thinking. "So get a real girlfriend."

He rolled to his back and clasped his hands over his chest. "It's not as easy as snapping my fingers."

"Why not? You're handsome. Kind. Not a serial killer. That I know of. And you're so successful."

"The money that success has earned me attracts the wrong kind of people."

"I get that. Never found a woman who can see the real you?"

"I wouldn't say that. I'm cautious about who I date so I've never had an issue with gold diggers. It's just—well…"

She sensed it was that issue of his. "Ozzy, you know how much my family loves you?"

"That's a different kind of love from romantic love, Lemon. I've taken to heart what you said about telling myself I'm unlovable. I really want to try to move beyond that."

She reached up and landed her hand on his shoulder. "Need any help from me?"

"You're already helping. You have it all together. You help others get it together. You've always got a smile on your face and are willing to help out when needed. And you play Bach like a master."

Where was he when she had been staring in the mirror checking her lack of confidence?

"I'll take 'have it all together' and enjoy it for the next few days." She tapped the word tattooed on his forearm. *Persevere.* Yes, that made sense. "This has been a dream couple of days. Living out the fantasy of being an islander. Getting to wear fancy clothes and treating this amazing home as my own."

"The lying part is a little squicky though."

"Wrong usage, but I get you. Little white lies are fine once in a while, but I don't like lying to your grandma. And with my parents arriving tonight…"

"It's just for a couple more days, Lemon. Though…now that I think about it, I doubt your mom would ever approve of me dating her daughter."

"Why not? Mom loves you, Ozzy."

"Maybe in a family love sort of way. But to hear that I'm dating her daughter? In a lovers' way? I'm not so sure she'd be pleased with that. Harry was dead against it."

A lovers' way. Mmm…yes, she could imagine her and Ozzy *not* partitioning themselves away from another on that big cozy bed. But not if her parents were anywhere near his bedroom. And Eliza was right next door!

"I think you'd be surprised," she said. "Mom knows my dating life is hit-and-miss, at best. I'm not a talented dater by any means. I can't do the going out to the bar or club thing. Hookups are not my love language. I like to be fixed up by someone I know. The guy's gotta be vetted by a friend. That's the only way I can feel comfortable."

"I'll be vetting Dimitri for you."

"And don't forget it. Can you give me any hints? Clues? Is he handsome? Talented? Rich?"

"All of the above, Lemon, I promise. I should go check on Amaris." He sat up, and Lennon felt as though she'd scared him off with questions about Dimitri. Why had she even asked? She already didn't care if the romance with a stranger ever came to fruition.

He tapped the violin case. "Can I make a request?"

"Try me." Lennon grabbed her violin and scooted to the bed's edge.

"How about some AC/DC?"

"Oh yeah?" Did he think he could stump her? Not Lennon Hart, first chair violinist and secret heavy metal enthusiast. Lennon bowed into the opening strains of "Thunderstruck."

Ozzy raised his arms and made horns with his fingers, banging his head as he strode to the door. He started singing when she reached the chorus. It was the weirdest thing to find herself standing in Ozzy Wilder's bedroom playing heavy metal on her violin.

But also, she could do this every day, with him.

CHAPTER THIRTEEN

When her parents arrived on the front lawn of Ozzy's property, Lennon shoved her brother aside to give her mom a big bear hug. Her dad joined in and enveloped them both and then Harry piled on. A Hart family hug. They were the best.

"It's been less than a week since I've seen you, sweetie." Her mom tousled her hair. "You're beaming. This Greek air must be something else."

It was something else. Having just left Ozzy's bedroom after playing an impromptu heavy metal violin solo for him, Lennon was still walking on clouds.

"How was the flight?" Lennon, along with Harry, grabbed their parents' luggage, and they all strolled up the walk. "Did you see the white caves on the drive here? Look at that water! It's like a dreamland here. I'm never leaving."

"That can be arranged." Ozzy stepped out from the front door with a side wink to Lennon. Both her parents pulled him into a hug.

After what seemed like ten minutes of hugs, tears and happy greetings, Ozzy directed her parents to their bedroom to unpack. And she walked backward—right into Ozzy's hug from behind. His big strong hands clasped in front of her belly. And he nuzzled against the crown of her head. "Uh…?"

"I love your parents, Lemon."

"They love you." She placed her hands on his. So strong and— Did he realize how intimate this hug actually was? "Uh, there's no one around."

"I think I'm still riding the hug high," he said against her ear. "I don't want it to end. Your parents rock."

If the man knew what his deep tenor did to her inhibitions. And feeling his hard muscles against all parts of her that desperately wanted that hot romance. Now! And that was clue that she needed to not lean against him, and extricate herself before something irreversible happened. Something completely uncharacteristic of Lennon Hart. Like mauling the man with an unasked for kiss.

"So!" Lennon spun out of the hug and went to the fridge to find—nothing in particular. "Beach party tonight?"

"Uh, yeah." She noticed he held his arms in front of himself uncomfortably, then finally dropped them at his sides. Missing their hug?

Get in line, buddy. "You tell your mom and dad about, er, us?"

"Heading to their room right now to spill the tea." Lennon sighed then lifted her shoulders. "I can do this."

"Of course you can. You're the manifestation guru, the queen of dorks, the maestro of heavy metal. You can do anything, Lemon."

"Maestro of heavy metal?" She gestured dismissively and wandered past him. "Chill, honeybun. Save the flattery for when it's required."

"It wasn't meant as flattery," he muttered as she passed him. "You really impress me, Lemon."

She picked up her pace to end that awkward exchange. Because every minute she spent in Ozzy's presence, her goal to manifest a summer romance altered. Because, what if, just maybe it wasn't some island friend he introduced her to but instead…him?

A bonfire blazed out on the beach. Lennon sorted through her things that hung on a standing rack in Ozzy's closet, looking for something comfy to wear. They'd eaten lobster and shrimp for supper, not dinner, and she was stuffed. It had felt like a family reunion with Eliza and Ozzy and her parents and Harry and— Claire was arriving tomorrow.

After eating, her mom had given Ozzy another

long hug and kissed his cheek, telling him how happy she was that he was dating her daughter. Really. After telling her parents that she and Ozzy had begun dating they'd initially laughed. But then her mom's laughter had stopped. She'd looked to her dad. They'd both nodded. And then announced they were happy for her. Like, for *real*. Mom had even said something to the effect that it was about time Ozzy realized how long Lennon had been pining for him.

She had never pined. Not out in the open, so people could see.

Though, if her mom had known as much…?

Didn't matter. They had bought the ruse. And much as it killed Lennon to lie to them, it also buoyed her in a surprising manner. Her dad had never been so excited when learning who she was dating. He genuinely loved Ozzy as much as the rest of the family.

If only Ozzy could be aware of how loved he truly was.

After pulling on blue culottes and a shirt, she grabbed her phone and wandered out through the kitchen. Destination: an evening of family fun.

Scrolling to check her comments, Lennon paused as she entered the living area. Ozzy walked inside with—a baby in his arms? What the…? She glanced about, searching for the source of—a baby?

He strolled into the kitchen and opened the fridge while simultaneously gently bouncing the infant.

"Um, Ozzy?"

He closed the fridge door and set a can of pop on the counter next to Eliza's list of last-minute touches to the cake. "What's up? Are you heading out to the bonfire? That color is awesome on you."

Lifted by the compliment and his throaty tone, Lennon performed a little swish from side to side. "Thank you. But, uh, do you need help with that?"

"With the pop?" He pushed it toward her. "Thanks." He went back to cradling the baby with both hands, rocking a bit, eyeing it directly and smiling at it.

Lennon snapped open the can and shoved it back toward him. She had meant help with *the baby*. What altered universe had she stepped into? "So, uh, where did you get that baby?"

"Claire's sister Chrissy and her husband Keith just arrived. Chrissy looked frazzled and she gratefully handed over this little one when I offered to help. I think her name is Carmelina. I'm calling her Carmel."

"Carmel?"

"I didn't hear the exact name because Chrissy was sniffing back tears. I think she's had a long day of it, especially traveling with an infant. Carmel here is fresh out of the oven. Only been a month. You're such a pretty little girl," he cooed at the baby, who held his eye contact in the wide-eyed marvel that made babies so irresistible. "And look at the pretty dress with the dragonflies on it. You're a princess."

Seeing Ozzy holding a baby was even more mind-blowing than the amazing acceptance she'd just received from her parents. But really? If he wanted to convince Amaris of his family values…

"I can give you a hand with that very fragile baby if you want me to."

She held out her arms. Not that he looked like he needed help. He'd clearly done this before—but when had he ever held a baby?

Wait. He had mentioned something about babysitting, but then had clammed up, not wanting to expound. Curiouser and curiouser.

"You think I'm going to break her?" he asked. "I know what I'm doing, Lemon. Remember I told you I babysat for a while? Back when I was twelve or thirteen."

"You said not to ask about it." The idea of Ozzy—rather the gawky yet charming teenager he had been—as a babysitter was adorable.

"Harry doesn't even know about it. I never told you guys because it seemed kind of uncool. I did it for a neighbor on Grandma's street one summer. Made some good money."

He had hidden that well. If she'd known about it at the time, it would have utterly exploded Lennon's crush on the guy. Her teenage heart may not have been able to handle all the feels.

What to do with this information? It was as though the gods of attraction had just blasted him with a supercharged bolt of lightning that seemed to sparkle all around him and a neon sign glinted Husband Material above his head.

"Just run out and have some fun, will you, Lemon? Me and Carmel are going to look out the window at the pretty blue ocean. I'll be out after she goes down for the night." He devolved into cooing baby talk and strolled past her.

Mouth hanging open, Lennon marveled for a moment over the transformation of her fake boyfriend from sexy closet hustler to ultrasexy daddy material. And he'd never be able to deny it either. "Last chance for some assistance," she called.

"We're good!"

"Alrighty then."

Best she leave him be. Because if she stood there one moment longer that goal of finding romance with another man would be completely obliterated. Only to be solidly replaced by Ozzy Wilder, the guy she was falling for all over again.

CHAPTER FOURTEEN

OZZY HAD NEVER excelled at the family games he'd been invited to when he was younger. The Hart family was big into them, so when Harry had told him to order the burlap bags for the three-legged sack race, he'd done so.

Bonfire crackling in the background, everyone was partnered up, including Mr. and Mrs. Hart, members of the wedding party and guests who wanted to take part in the race. Carmel was asleep inside, her parents wielding a baby monitor. When they wanted to join in, Eliza helpfully took charge of the monitor.

With a glance to the far room in the villa where an inner light beamed, he saw Amaris Chastain watching. He waved and she waved back. Big family man moment here. But the idea of making a show of it quickly vanished. Just being around the Harts changed his attitude. He never felt the need to prove himself to them.

Yeah, Ozzy, so why does it matter what any-

one else thinks? Start believing new things, as Lemon told you.

"You ready for this?" Lemon playfully waved a sack as if she were a matador teasing the bull. "If there's one game I can win, it's the potato sack race."

"Load me in, Lemon."

They each put a leg in the sack and managed a wobbling walk over to the start line alongside the other couples. Bodies hugging, he wondered if his extra foot of height over her petite form was going to be an issue. He could probably lift the sack, bringing her feet off the ground, and carry her for her light weight.

Heh. That would be cheating. And not as intimate as having to hug her close against his body as they tried to get their connected legs in step.

"You ready?"

He tugged up the burlap bag. "As I'll ever be."

Eliza shouted the command to "Go!" and everyone took off in a burst of adrenaline and laughter.

"Arm around me!" Lemon directed his hand around her waist, and she hugged him in turn. "That's the key. Stay close."

They quickly found a rhythm. And from what he could see, they were in the lead along with Harry and Claire's sister.

"You think we should let the groom win?" he asked.

"Are you crazy? This! Is! Sparta!" Lemon charged.

Chuckling and holding her tightly he dialed into her warrior vibe and they overtook their competition. Lemon called out that they were *losers*. Harry shouted back that they were cheating.

Hardly. Ozzy could barely focus on moving his leg forward in time with Lemon's because she was so…there. Hugged up alongside him. Body moving against his. Her laughter moved her tiny breast against his chest, and he got a zing of arousal that no man wanted to deal with at a moment like this.

A flash of the evil eye from Harry redirected the blood that had started to flow downward and back to his extremities. Back in the game.

As they crossed the finish line, Lemon thrust up her arms in triumph. Ozzy stumbled. Sensing he might trip over her, he quickly wrapped his arms around her body and made sure she went down on top of him instead of beneath his weight.

Spilling onto the sand, her giggles erupted and they sparked his own laughter. When Lemon pressed her hands into the sand on either side of his head to lean away from him, he slid a hand along her cheek. Bonfire light glowed across her skin, dancing in her eyes. The flames brightened her hair. Beautiful. Unique. Luminous. Her chest shook against his as her laughter slowly ebbed and she bowed her forehead to his shoulder.

Wrapping his arms across her back, Ozzy held her there, hearts racing against one another. His fingers teased through her hair and the press of her small breasts against his chest stirred him again. It felt like a moment for a kiss…

Lemon locked gazes with him. “Oh.”

A simple “Oh.” It was the truest statement spoken. Because yes. Just, *oh.* Was he going to allow his teenage angst to stop him from kissing the girl again? Lemon was right. He kept calling himself unlovable, when he was surrounded by people who genuinely loved and cared for him.

“Lemon, I…” *Want to believe I can be loved.* Maybe a kiss could change everything…

As other couples arrived across the finish line, Angela Hart bent near Ozzy’s and Lemon’s heads. “Good going, you two.”

Her voice broke the enchantment. Ozzy slid his hand from Lemon’s hair and he sat up, which caused Lemon to tumble, her leg tangled in the bag. He reached to help her, but the move toppled him and they both faced sand, laughing.

“Need some help?” Harry called.

“Let the lovebirds alone,” one of the groomsmen said.

Lovebirds? Clearly, they were playing their parts well. Maybe a little too well, because he'd had the thought to kiss her, despite their no kissing rule. Not that he really could have attempted a kiss in front of her family. Despite them believing they were a couple.

Mr. and Mrs. Hart had said they were happy that he and Lemon were dating. Hmm… If he shook off the insistent need to label himself unworthy, could he be good enough for Lemon?

Lemon finally managed to twist her way to sitting position and extract her leg from the bag. As the racers wandered back to the bonfire, Ozzy pulled off the bag and stood. He offered Lemon a hand and with a tug, he pulled her fairy weight up. She landed with a bounce next to him.

Finding themselves alone, he brushed the hair from her face and lingered on the softness of her skin against the back of his fingers. Heaving breaths lifted her chest and they both laughed. Had he ever laughed with a woman before, forgotten himself? It was nice. Real.

"We work well together," she said.

"On a lot of things." He retracted his touch from her. "Sorry."

"It's okay." She took his hand and clasped it between both of hers. "You've got the warmest touch. Kind of makes a girl feel…" She shrugged. "Loved."

"Yeah, well, uh…"

What to say to that? And he wanted to start facing that he had romantic feelings for Lemon. The woman he was supposed to introduce to someone else in a few days.

"Move off the finish line you two!" someone called. "We're going for another race."

Ozzy slid his arm across Lemon's shoulders, and they wandered away from the finish line. "We'd better get back to the games."

"Sure. Wouldn't want anyone to think we're out here…"

"Being boyfriend and girlfriend?"

"Right?"

Her hopeful tone echoed in his heart. All Lemon wanted was an affair that turned into love?

Could Ozzy Wilder have romantic love?

CHAPTER FIFTEEN

LENNON WOKE AND stretched out an arm, then remembered her sleeping partner and flinched back. They'd both tumbled into bed after an evening of beach games. It had been crazy fun. Even, sexy. When she'd landed on top of Ozzy in the sand and he had held her, not speaking, just…feeling. It had been a moment.

Her teenage fantasies about Ozzy had never gone that far or felt so real.

Carefully, she sat up, only to find Ozzy's side of the bed was empty. No one sleeping on the chaise in the closet either.

What time was it? Grabbing her phone, she saw it was after 2:00 a.m. Plopping her head onto the pillow and closing her eyes, she wished herself back to sleep, but her thoughts hummed.

Ozzy and a baby. Talk about adding to his weapons of mass seduction. The way he'd held that baby and carried her around, cooing and bouncing her, she had to suspect he would make a terrific dad. Juxtaposing the sexy charmer with the soft, gentle father image did things to her libido. Dang, that man had wriggled back into her heart. And sleeping next to him wasn't helping her willpower. Because even in his absence, she could smell his ocean and sand scent, so overwhelming, almost protective. But also, teasing.

With a sigh, she got up and padded barefoot down the dark hallway toward the kitchen, dimly lit by a stream of moonlight.

A brighter light caught her eye, and she followed it to the opened fridge. "Ozzy?" she whispered.

The man popped his head up, spoon hanging from his mouth. "Lemon," he muttered around the utensil. He pulled it out. "Are you spying on me?"

"No. I just woke and needed a drink. What are you— Are you eating your grandma's buttercream? That's supposed to go on the wedding cake!"

"She won't mind," he said in a loud whisper.

He closed the fridge and they stood in semidarkness—he in only a pair of plaid boxers and she in her concert T-shirt and shorts. So stylish. Not. But his steely abs woke her up completely. Lennon had never touched a real six-pack beyond the kind a person bought from a liquor store. She curled her fingers into her palms.

The sweet scent of the frosting drew her closer. "That smells good."

Ozzy offered his spoon, a dab of white frosting on the end of it. She ate it.

"You've never had anything better, right?" he whispered.

"Oh my God, I'm in heaven. But Eliza will kill you."

He held up a little plastic tub. "We have this unspoken agreement, me and Grandma. I won't mess with her batch stuff if she leaves me a little treat. Been going on since I was a kid. Trust me. She wants me to have this." His wink was visible in the muggy moonlight. "Grab a spoon. Let's go out to the balcony."

Lennon opened the silverware drawer. "I'm right behind you."

Ozzy settled onto a double-wide chaise and patted the cushion next to him. Lennon had no qualms about snuggling up close, legs bent and shoulder nudging his. Because: frosting! But also, they'd developed an easy closeness since the beach games. Not snuggle-up-in-bed close. Or casually touch-his-abs close. Yet.

She aimed her spoon for the tub he held. "I'm supposed to be getting a drink of water and quietly drifting back to sleep. The sugar content of this stuff will have me wide-eyed for the rest of the night."

"Worth the sacrifice," he said, with another dip of his spoon into the frosting. "You have trouble sleeping? That bed is so comfortable."

"Oh, it is. Like clouds and kitten fur. For the bed alone, you might have a tough time kicking me out after Harry is hitched. My mind was buzzing. I think with all that's gone on this week it's unavoidable. What about you?"

"Yeah, well, I was lying there…" He paused with the spoon in his mouth, and his eyes drifted over her face. It wasn't a cursory look. Lennon felt as if he were stripping her bare with his eyes and touching her in a way only a lover could. Sort of how she'd felt when he'd touched her cheek on the beach. "…next to you," he finally said, "and…let's just say I had to take a walk."

"Oh." She thought about that one. No. He couldn't have been. Turned on by her? Had he… wanted to touch her as much as she now wanted to stroll her tongue up and down his abs? "So you were…thinking things about me?"

He nodded. "It's complicated, Lemon. Sharing a bed. I'm not used to…faking it." He spooned another dab of buttercream into his mouth. "I mean, I've never had a woman just *sleep* beside me."

"Interesting," Lennon declared.

He gave her a side glance. "That's it? Interesting?"

She *couldn't* tell him it made her day—or night—to know he might have been having sexy thoughts about her. Their sleeping situation hadn't been meant as a means to hook up with the man. And really, she'd gone into this fake girlfriend role with the confidence that she was over him. He'd broken her teenage heart. She wouldn't allow it to happen to her grown-up, kind of, sort of mature heart.

Who was she kidding? *Break away, Oscar Wilder. Break. A. Way.* And if she was really serious about keeping him at arm's length then… She looked at their close proximity. Arms and legs hugging, an easy snuggle. This was obviously the "sort of" part of her mature heart.

"I'd be upset if you didn't have such thoughts," she said.

"Lemon." Ozzy shifted to face her. He spooned another dab of the delicious treat and offered it to her. "Do you think I'm attractive?" He held the spoon closer to her. She focused beyond it to his eyes.

"Are you being serious right now?" She snatched the frosting with a quick bite. "You may think you're a dork, but your outsides scream sexy. I mean, those abs alone are worth a full chapter in a romance novel."

He stabbed his spoon at the frosting. "I think *you're* sexy."

Another spoon of frosting was offered, but Lennon's mouth fell open. She was unable to process that statement. He thought she was... Skinny, no curves, awkward, and not as confident as she faked it to her followers? He found *that* sexy?

"Well, there's proof that you're sleep-deprived," she said to him. "No one has ever called me that."

But hearing it felt like a validation. Another chip at that self-esteem issue that had only ever put her in the dork girl category. Could he know how much she needed to hear that?

"Then no one has ever seen you the way I do." He handed her the tub.

If she grabbed him and started making out with him right now—no. It felt like a make out moment, but something held her back. She was only just realizing she wanted him. And he was still falling on the side of being unlovable.

"You know I've never brought a woman here to my home on Zakynthos?"

"I find that surprising. This is a dream getaway. Uber romantic. The perfect place to bring a woman you care about." He'd brought *her* here. In a manner.

No, Lennon, don't confuse this fake with what you want to manifest. You're smarter than that!

"I've never found anyone that I wanted to spend time with here, alone, and far from the rush of Paris." He sighed. "Honestly? I think I protect my heart too much. That's sad, isn't it?"

A little. But look at her, doing much the same! "You're being open with me right now. And I understand your need to keep others out."

"You do?"

"It's to do with being sent to live with your grandma, isn't it? About feeling like your parents never loved you?"

"Yes, but I've been questioning that lately. You told me I've given myself this label of unlovable."

"You're not unlovable, Ozzy."

"I really am trying to wrap my head around that. Not blame my emotionless-dating history on that label. Maybe I just don't know *how* to do romance."

Yes, if only there were an instruction manual!

"I feel you. I could be in the same boat. I don't have anyone either. And it's because I've always been unable to trust that a guy truly loves me."

"You've got me, Lemon." He leaned over and dipped a finger into the frosting and licked it off.

Mercy.

Did she have him? Did she want him? What was he doing to her right now? Turning the tables and making this feel like…seduction. Because all parts of her were loosening, relaxing, wanting to touch, to taste…

Lennon didn't know how to process this. The

man was breaking their rules. Not that they'd made rules regarding the fake. Save for no kisses. But she had her personal rules about— Really? She didn't have any rules. And she really didn't need *this* in the middle of the night. No way would she sleep now knowing Ozzy Wilder actually thought she was sexy.

The only way to survive the next few days would be to keep her distance. Focus on the goal: romance. With someone else.

She stood and sighed. "You've got me for another day or two. I gotta get back to bed or I'll have a sleep hangover all day tomorrow."

She rushed back into the house, but a glance back saw Ozzy brush his hands over his hair and shake his head.

Was he…had he…? Did he *like* her? He'd once told her they could never date. *Ever.*

But as well, he had said he'd liked her while standing on the curb that night. So those feelings—might they still exist for her?

Carp. How to process this? She'd arrived on the island, eager to manifest a hot summer romance. Had she actually manifested one between her and Ozzy Wilder?

CHAPTER SIXTEEN

THE DAY BEFORE the big event the wedding planner, along with a two-person crew, breezed in and took control. Ozzy was thankful to hand the supervisory reins over to her.

After grabbing a can of pop from the fridge, he gave his grandma a kiss on the cheek. She stood before an arrangement of cake parts on the vast marble counter. "Need some help?"

"Absolutely not. This cake will come together like a dream. But you can do me a favor and check on her." She gestured toward the living area and Ozzy noticed Lemon sitting on the sofa before a window, her head bowed over her phone. "She's been muddling for a while."

"Thanks, Grandma. Claire's arriving later today. I'm sure the bride will be excited about the cake."

"I want to have it all put together before she gets here, so scoot! Take care of your sweetheart."

"Right." His sweetheart.

Or? Someone he might really want to get involved with after living with her for a few days and experiencing everything Lemon. Easy. Interesting. More fun than he'd had with any other woman. And they got each other in a manner where they didn't have to speak or circle around not speaking. Those handholds and reassuring squeezes from her meant so much. She had shown him how to do quiet. How to lay beside a woman in his bed and just…be thankful for her presence.

But did she still expect him to fix her up after the wedding? A hot summer romance? Kind of felt as though they were having one right now. Lukewarm? At least, they were trying it out in an attempt to fool the others. The faking it part had already taxed his morals too much. Would she consider him as possible date material? Capable of romance?

Did *he* believe he could sweep Lemon off her feet? According to Lemon, belief was what was required.

"Lemon." He settled onto the sofa opposite, bringing up his legs so their bare feet touched. He pressed his toes to hers. "What's up with the frown? Have a buttercream hangover?"

That got a smile from her. "I'm going to eat that whole cake she's putting together in the kitchen. So I'm warning you now to please hold me back."

"What if I'm right there with you diving in with forks?"

"Pretty sure Claire will not be having that."

Ozzy shrugged and wiggled his toes against hers. "I'll take that arrow."

When had he ever played footsie with a woman? Could she think of him as a man she wanted to date as opposed to simply a man who was acting as a pseudo-boyfriend in preparation for a real one? Or had he already spoiled any chance of that happening? Should he have waited and given her the necklace *after* she'd helped him? It looked so good around her neck. She deserved that and so much more for helping him with this crazy fake.

Her morose expression bothered him. "Grandma says you've been sulking for a while. What's going on in that cute little brain of yours?"

"First. My brain is not little."

"My bad. You are one hell of a smart chick."

"Thank you. As for the sulk." She shrugged and handed him her phone. "I accidentally posted a pic of us on the yacht. It's never been so dreadful to read comments before. They are not stellar."

He took the phone, which was open to her Tik-

Tok account, and scrolled through some of the comments.

Is she a gold digger?

How did she ever snatch a sexy god like that?

The new clothes are not her style. Something is off.

Is she a big fake? She did not manifest him!

When did she become okay with lying to us?

The words, though he knew were from strangers, and probably even bots, tugged at his heart. He could imagine what they did to Lemon's soft and squishy heart. None of it was true. And yet, *he* had asked her to lie for him.

It hurt his heart to realize that he was using Lemon that way. He'd bought her those clothes. Had he inadvertently brought on some of that hate?

He wanted to protect Lemon and give her everything that would make her happy. To see her smile because that was her natural state not because some strangers approved of her reels. He wanted her…to look at him the way he looked at her. As a potential partner. And it was time he started giving how to make that happen some good thought.

He handed the phone back to her. “You know those people don’t really know you?”

“I know. It’s the yacht. Such a luxury. Everyone glommed onto that image and started picking it apart. Being an influencer is not for the faint of heart. And I’ve never thought I was that faint. But…” She exhaled and her shoulders curved forward. “I am lying to them about manifesting the nice clothes. And I could explain you’re just a friend but… Amaris. I don’t think she’ll find my TikTok but if she did, I don’t want her to think anything but that we’re a couple. Oh, Ozzy, I’m a fake!”

“Hey.” He shuffled forward and pulled her in for a hug. She melted against him and he nuzzled his face into her hair, fully aware his grandma stood across the room, but not caring to put on an act for anyone right now. “Lemon.”

“Ozzy.” Such a soft whisper of dejection.

He winced against her hair. No one had a right to make his girl feel so bad. And why? Because of him. He had put her in the position where she felt she had to conceal the truth in order to help him. What a jerk!

“Do you want to stop this fake act right now? Because I don’t want to do anything to hurt you. And if those comments upset you…”

"I don't want to stop this—what we've got going on." She lingered in his gaze, and he wondered if she was feeling the same attraction as he did. "I'm happy to help you and Eliza. It's just the comments about me not being able to attract someone like you really do hurt."

"You know those people only say hurtful things because they can't exist unless they make others miserable?"

"I know that. I really do. Here I thought I was so confident. Ready to take on that last big hurdle of finding love."

"Nothing has changed, Lemon. You are that confident woman. Keep telling yourself that. And you will find love. I think you're too close to see the truth."

"What does that mean?"

"It means I see a beautiful woman with a bright personality who is able to win over anyone she talks to. My grandma, for one. Even Amaris. You've got more talent than any of us can dream to have. You kick ass with the violin. And you are always trying to help others through your online presence."

"I do enjoy learning when others have manifested things into their lives."

"And you told me it's not magic. Manifesting works because you act toward the thing you desire." Ozzy paused.

Yes, that thing he desired. Which was Lemon. Right now she smelled like softness and sand. The freckles on her face teased. Her wondering gaze tickled at his sense of propriety. A kiss felt imminent.

No, he couldn't risk it with his grandma so close. A first kiss should be perfect. And who was he to think he could be perfect for Lemon? But he could help her with the negative comments.

"Give me your phone."

She slapped it onto his palm.

"No social media today or tomorrow. Only use your phone to take photos of the wedding. Deal?"

She winced. He knew it was a big ask. Especially for someone whose job depended on her being connected.

"The people who are really interested in you and who enjoy your content will not disappear in two days, Lemon. Promise." He set her phone on the coffee table. "I think I know what you need. A reset. And there's a place close by that will change your religion. Let me take you out to Lover's Cove."

"What?"

"It's a surreal place with blue water and white rocks. I promise it'll make you stop thinking about all things online."

"Lover's Cove." A big exhale lifted and dropped

her shoulders, then she nodded. Defeated? He didn't like seeing her in a slump. But she rallied and gave him a weak smile. "Let's do it."

"That's my Lemondrop."

They took a motorboat out to what Ozzy called Lover's Cove. Better known as the Blue Caves. Lennon stretched out on the padded bow of the boat and took in the brilliant blue sky. The Midwest got some pretty skies, but the Greek skies she'd experienced the past few days rivaled Minnesota's sunniest, puffy-clouds day.

When the motor shut off, she turned onto her stomach and took in the tall, surreal white limestone shoreline, carved into arches by water lapping against it. Like something a person might see in a fantasy movie set on a faraway planet. A stretch of her arm tipped her fingers in the ultrablue water. She almost expected it to have a blueberry flavor due to the color. One quick lick. Not fruity.

"Those rocks have eroded over the ages," Ozzy said from his seat by the motor. "They reflect the water and turn it into a fantasyland."

They were on the same mental track. And that he'd thought she needed a reset was so thoughtful. Darn it, she did have confidence! And no faceless online comments were going to bring her down. Bring on the romance. Lennon Hart was in it to win it.

She hadn't specified that Ozzy *couldn't* be in the running for her manifestation. Of course, that had been when she'd landed firmly on the "I will never trust Ozzy again" side.

Now? Dare she make it real?

"Everything about Greece is a fantasyland," she said. "I'm going to do my best to smuggle myself in a guest room after the wedding. See how long it takes you to notice I didn't leave."

Ozzy laughed. "I'd offer you the bungalow, but I asked Grandma to stay as long as she likes."

"Really? That's awesome. I love that you and your grandma are so close."

"She's the best parent I've known. And with her getting older I want to make sure she's looked after. No nursing homes for her. I want her to move here permanently if she will. I'll even hire an on-site caregiver for her if it ever comes to that."

"What about when you're in Paris?"

"I own a penthouse in the 6th arrondissement. The whole building, actually. I'm sure there's an open apartment just below me that Grandma would love. But let me convince her to make a permanent move first."

"I hope she does. And just think, buttercream frosting whenever you want!"

"Oh yeah."

The boat floated under a white limestone arch. Sunlight danced on the water. As they closely passed the stone wall, Lennon brushed her fingertips across the rough, dry surface. Another boat about a hundred yards away was filled with people.

"Tourist season," Ozzy said. "You can swim or dive in the inner caves. But boats aren't allowed in for that reason."

"I've never been diving."

"I'll take you if you intend to stick around after the wedding."

"I'd…" Love to do that. But didn't he remember that she wanted him to introduce her to a potential romance? She wanted to forget about that request. So maybe she would let his offer stand. "I'd come here every day if I lived this close. You live in such a beautiful place, Ozzy."

"I still prefer Paris."

She turned to rest on her elbows and swung an astonished look toward him. "I don't know. The Eiffel Tower is cool, but this?"

"I could show you some amazing sights in Paris. All the places the tourists don't know about. I'd even take you to the Opera to see a symphony."

Lennon lay back again, marveling as they passed under another arch of sun-bleached stone.

"I'd like to see Paris." And to see a symphony with Ozzy? What a dream! "You're very lucky to have a home in both countries."

"Paris makes me happy. Greece relaxes me."

"Who would have thought designing closets could make a guy so rich."

"Right? And all thanks to me seeking a hideout in my grandma's closet when I was a kid."

"Tell me more about that."

"After my parents' divorce I was freaked by life in general. You know…well…" He huffed out a heavy exhale and shrugged. "I used to sit in my grandma's fancy closet and cry. It took me a long time to get over the fact my parents weren't interested in raising me. What was so wrong with me that meant they couldn't bear to be around their own son? Still may not be completely over that fact."

A lump rose in her throat to hear the pain in his voice. "When I was younger, I don't think I fully understood how devastating that was for you. I think you landed in a good place though."

"Grandma is the best. She was the one who supported my career dreams and took me in at a point where she should have had the freedom to adventure. I owe her a lot."

"I don't think she needs you to pay her back monetarily. Eliza doesn't strike me as the sort."

"She's not. Money doesn't mean much to her.

That's why I believe the gesture of getting back Cozy Closets will be the best repayment I can give her."

"Maybe." Lennon was beginning to wonder if maybe Eliza couldn't care less about Cozy Closets. She seemed happy doing her thing, baking the occasional cake, and now, with plans to move to Greece, she might enjoy retirement relaxing on the beach.

"As for me?" Ozzy stretched out his legs and tilted his head back to take in the sun. "All that cash and yet, still alone."

Lennon sat up and caught her elbows on her knees. "You'll find the one someday."

"What about you? Do you think you'll ever leave Tangle Lake? Start following your dreams?"

She hadn't had such extravagant dreams until she'd flown to Greece and had stepped into Ozzy's world. "Never say never."

"I've a guest room for you whenever you want to stay, Lemon."

"Don't think I won't take you up on that offer."

"I hope you will."

"But I intend to move to a hotel after the wedding. Might be weird if I stayed on while indulging in my hot summer romance."

"Oh, right. Sure. Dimitri. I think he'll match your dork level. But we're not going to discuss your future love life right now." He moved up from the back of the boat to sit on a side seat, the position putting him knee-to-knee with her. "I like spending time with you. The last time I took off in the boat just to look at these caves was, well, never."

"You must spend time with friends." She leaned forward, tracing his sharp jaw with a gaze. "Always busy doing things?"

"My friends are all in Paris. It's a little boring here, if I'm being truthful, but I do love the air and sea."

His face had hardened to sharp angles and was softened with the tousle of hair. But never had his gaze been so intense, so focused on her. "You've changed, Ozzy."

"How so?"

She touched his jaw. Gently. Contact felt necessary.

"You used to be the quiet cool kid with the aloof attitude and a charm that most girls couldn't figure out yet would fall all over you anyway. Like you didn't care if a girl swooned over you or not. The whole population of girls in the school were yours for the taking. But you've gotten..." Sexier. More present. Downright feastable. She tapped his jaw. "Mysterious."

Ozzy chuckled. "I think you watch too many of those romance movies, Lemon. Aloof and mysterious?"

"It's an attractive combination." She leaned back, catching the heels of her hands behind her. "I posted a reel on how to attract your dream mate last year by acting *as if* it had already happened."

"Did it work for you?"

"Well. I mean… I try to keep the reels lighthearted. I'm not promising anything, for sure."

"I thought this summer romance manifestation thing was for real? Wasn't that your goal? Find a man. Stir in some romance. Happily-ever-after?"

"I'm not sure I mentioned happily-ever-after."

"Sounded like it when we were talking about our hopes to get married someday."

He remembered so much about their conversations. The man really listened.

Ozzy leaned over the boat's prow. A push against the white rocky wall steered the boat away from a crash into it. "I hope I can find someone who makes me as happy as Claire makes Harry."

"They are a perfect fit for one another. Her airy bohemian nature balances Harry's go-get-'em corporate raider tendencies. As for you, you'll find your fit soon enough."

"Promise?"

The ache in that single word poked at her heart.

"I can't make any promises," she said carefully. "You have to manifest your life the way you desire."

"Yeah. Manifesting..." His attention veered across the water.

She toyed with the fat lemon diamond at the base of her throat. She'd never thought she'd be taking such a close look at her feelings with Ozzy while playing his girlfriend. On the other hand, the practice she'd thought to gain by agreeing to this fake was exposing a side of him that she'd never known. That he was being real with her meant so much. It felt like a gift.

Ozzy moved to sit beside her, and they both laid back to stare up at the sky.

"I'll always be your friend," she said softly. Though it summoned a tear to say, "Whenever you need me, I'll be there." Because she wanted so much more than friendship.

"Thanks, Lemon. Ditto." His hand found hers in a clasp. "As for the manifesting... I'm going to give it a try."

"Good for you."

As the boat floated, the two of them seemed to leave the fantasy of the blue waters and white rocks behind. Ozzy's eyes locked on to Lennon's. Feeling in her body, but also away from it, she couldn't comprehend what to do. To touch him again? *Yes, please.* To stroke the swag of dark hair from his forehead? *Uh-huh.* Yet she couldn't move. Everything felt so perfect, like one wrong move would bring it all crashing down.

Never had she felt so connected, so deeply embraced by a man. Without even touching. This was more than a friendship. It had to be. And she'd been telling herself she preferred Ozzy in place of that mystery man he intended to set her up with. The risk could be worth it. Rocking softly on the water. So far from home. Her and Ozzy. The boy, the man, who had stolen her heart.

And she wasn't sure she wanted it returned.

Ozzy was the first to break the spell by sitting up with a heavy sigh. "We'd better head back. Claire should be arriving soon."

"Of course." Lennon placed a hand on her chest. It was still there, her heart. But as Ozzy positioned himself back by the motor and fired it up, she felt sure a little piece of her had stowed away with him.

CHAPTER SEVENTEEN

CLAIRE'S ARRIVAL CARRIED the air of a royal returning to the castle. Lennon giggled over the buzz of the bridesmaids as they scurried out to meet their queen. Cheers, tears and bouncing hugs ensued. Harry, looking proud and a little teary-eyed himself, rushed out to spin his bride into a hug.

After she'd settled with Harry in their room, Claire breezed through the buttercream-scented house, eyed the cake like she was surveying a work of art and gave Eliza a big hug. Lennon caught the moment on video and decided to follow her around since the wedding photographer was only going to be here on the day. Whatever she recorded could turn into a nice memory for Harry and Claire. She was still observing Ozzy's request she avoid social media.

Photo ops were found as Claire approved of the altar setup. And the dance floor that had been erected on the beach gave Claire a swoon until she noticed the flowers draped there by the florists were English roses and not the bigger peace variety of roses she'd ordered. Was it possible to get replacements? It almost felt like a bridezilla moment, but Ozzy had swept in and said "Sure, no problem." The bride had sighed and hugged him.

Lennon's heart pitter-pattered at the heroic rescue. It was a big expense to have roses flown in overnight. Good ole Ozzy.

Around the time Harry convinced his fiancée to take a break with a swim in the pool, Lennon wandered into the kitchen where Eliza was tidying up after the late afternoon snack storm had vacated. She set her phone aside, recalling Ozzy's entreaty to not check her socials.

Eliza wrapped the boxes of leftover baking ingredients. "Lennon, would you be a dear and help me carry these boxes to the pantry?"

Lennon grabbed a few and followed her into the well-lit pantry that any person could make themselves at home in. Literally. It was as big as her bedroom.

Eliza showed her where to place the boxes and then sat on a chair. This had to be a Wilder's Wardrobes design. She hadn't realized Ozzy also did pantries. But, yes, she'd label this pantry sexy with the glass jars all aligned and neatly labeled, the cedar touches and hidden strip lighting that highlighted everything.

Then again, the man probably had the whole house made exactly to order.

Eliza took Lennon's hand and gave it a squeeze. "I'm glad Ozzy found someone to love with his whole heart."

Lennon didn't have to force a gentle smile. The lie was becoming easier. Almost an insistent truth. "That he has."

"I heard him get up last night," Eliza said. "Was it another nightmare? He hasn't had them in so long, I'd thought he was over them."

"A nightmare? Uh, no. He was just…couldn't sleep." Keeping the frosting sharing adventure a secret felt necessary. "What sort of nightmare?"

"He hasn't told you about them? I suppose not. He can be closed about some things."

He'd told her about hiding in his grandma's closet. Which she completely understood, given how his life had been upended. "He had nightmares when he stayed with you? Was it…because of his parents?"

Eliza adjusted a row of spices beside where she sat. She closed her eyes and nodded. "I'm sure he won't mind me telling you this, since the two of you are so close. Right after he moved in with me he'd wake in the middle of the night crying. I'd go in to comfort him, and he'd be in a partial sleep state, not completely awake. He'd mumble over and over, 'No one loves me.'" Eliza pressed a hand on her chest. "Broke my heart, the poor boy."

Lennon felt that sadness with a sudden tug at the corners of her eyes. "That is so sad. But you took him in. That was a huge responsibility. Ozzy mentioned you went back to work to support the both of you?"

"Yes, I opened my cake decorating business. After my husband died, I was left with enough to survive. But just when I thought I might be able to retire and start traveling with friends, Oscar came to live with me. His dad, my son, did help with finances, but the emotional part? I tried my best. I do hope he knows I love him."

"Oh, he does. He adores you, Eliza. Does he… ever speak to his parents? I haven't asked him much about them."

"I don't believe so. My son, Oscar's father, is very private. Heck, he'd prefer to pack up and move to the mountains and never see a single soul again if he didn't enjoy his day-trading so much. He lives in Manhattan. As for Oscar's mother, well…" Eliza shook her head. "She was very selfish. Always trying to be something she was not. You know, like those rich families on reality television. She was addicted to those shows. Always spending money on fancy shoes and even had a nose job. Though she did send Oscar cards for his birthday and Christmas. At least, for those first few years. Both of them were obviously never meant to be parents. But I would never say anything to Oscar. And you must never tell him I said so."

"I won't. Thank you for telling me that."

It explained a lot regarding Ozzy's need to pull away and that he hadn't settled into a romantic relationship. Was Ozzy capable of love? He seemed to still possess that little boy's broken heart. Though, certainly, he did love his grandma. And witnessing his tenderness with Carmel? He couldn't possibly still believe that no one could love him, could he?

"I adore your grandson." Truth.

"Then don't break his heart," Eliza said with a warning tone. "Promise me that."

Lennon nodded. Could she break a man's heart if she hadn't won it in the first place?

And now she thought on it…did she want to win his heart?

Everything inside her screamed yes, yes, and yes. That this fake dating thing had never really been fake.

CHAPTER EIGHTEEN

AFTER A VISIT with Amaris to find she was growing stir-crazy and had plans to slip out tomorrow while the festivities were taking place, Lennon wandered out to the beach. She hadn't gotten a read on Amaris, as to whether she was going to sell to Ozzy. During their interview, he'd pitched her an idea of how they would incorporate Cozy Closets but he hadn't told Lennon what that entailed. Lennon had mentioned how he'd wanted to hold the baby the moment he'd laid eyes on her.

Amaris's upper lip had curled. Really, *that* man, holding a baby?

Still not sold. Unfortunately.

They'd done their best. Had shown Amaris that Ozzy was in a relationship and surrounded by family. And it wasn't a lie. Not the family part.

Lennon plodded through the sand toward the bonfire, anger lifting at Amaris's stick-in-thc-mud attitude. Why did he have to prove himself to anyone? There was nothing wrong with a sexy closet. No one should discount him for a genius marketing campaign. Cozy Closets would find a perfect match should they allow Ozzy to buy.

Gathered around the bonfire, the wedding party shared beers, wine coolers and an assortment of fried, boiled and sauteed seafood. As the night grew long everyone shared stories of the bride and groom. After that, Claire and her bridesmaids shared worst dates ever.

Lennon yawned and slipped to the edge of the gathering. Led by the crescent moon in the velvet sky she wandered. If she never returned to Minnesota and its six months of winter—which meant no bare feet on the ground for half a year—she could be happy. Warm sand between one's toes was not as annoying as she'd initially thought. It was bliss.

Soon enough, her hand was clasped by Ozzy's sure grip. "Mind if I join you?"

"Not at all. You share your worst date with the crew?"

"I've been lucky. No burned leg hairs like Harry, and for sure haven't been puked on like Candace. What about you?"

"Well."

"Come on. Tell!"

"I had to pee once while my date was driving to an event in the country. In January. It was storming and the roads were glare ice. I got out, clinging to the car so I wouldn't slip and go down. Peed, and…slipped and landed right in it."

"Classic Minnesota winter dating hazard," Ozzy said with a chuckle.

"Right? My one pant leg had pee on it all through the party. Not the way to impress the guy, let me tell you."

"I'd have given you a spare pair of pants to change into. I always carried emergency snow gear in the trunk."

"I would have put on your crusty old sweatpants and been grateful."

"They probably were crusty. I only learned how to use the washer after I moved out of Grandma's place."

Lennon tilted her head against his shoulder. This was nice, the two of them, hand in hand, bare feet crushing the soft sand with their slow wander. "You ready to be the best man tomorrow?"

"I've been told that requires me making sure the groom doesn't get too drunk tonight. Claire had a firm conversation with me earlier."

"He's only had the one beer that I noticed. Harry isn't a big drinker."

"Yeah, but he's nervous. That's why I switched his out for NA beer."

"Sneaky, but effective."

"He'll do fine tomorrow. And I'll be there by

his side. As I expect him to be there for me someday. This week has been a nice preview to what my future could bring."

Lennon swallowed a gasp at that. Did he realize how that sounded? Well. She took it to mean he'd like *her* in his future.

"Same," she said, and stopped to turn toward the water. Not far off lay Ozzy's favorite log. The thought of it rippled a warm flush across her skin. Or maybe it was that Ozzy still held her hand. "I know this week has been busy and chaotic for you. Having to deal with Amaris and your grandma hasn't helped either. But it's been great for me. I'm glad I agreed to be your fake girlfriend."

"You got a lot of content to post. And soon enough you'll be starting your summer romance."

"Oh? Oh, right. I did want to manifest that," came out with not as much enthusiasm as she'd previously given it.

A few days ago she'd bounced giddily at the prospect of finding love. Now? It felt as though the air had been let out of her lungs. She couldn't imagine trying to impress a stranger or getting intimately involved with anyone unless—they called seashells remnants from a fairy steed.

If she put her heart out there, Ozzy would be kind with it. She knew that about him. Had witnessed his kindnesses toward others and herself.

And four days of faking it demanded she claw her way up from the mistruths and be real.

"You mean a lot to me, Ozzy. More than as a friend. I feel like we've become much closer. That whatever happened in the past is—well, I trust you now. What we have is..."

He stroked his fingers along her hairline. A lushly romantic move. She bowed her head toward his hand. Seeking him. Wanting to linger in this quiet moment. The gentle *shush* of water kissing the shore made it even more romantic.

The heat of him drew her like a moth. Did she still worry about getting singed? *No, absolutely not.*

"I know we've become close, Lemon. I've enjoyed every moment."

"You have?" came out as a desperate but relieved whisper. "Ozzy..."

She closed her eyes. Swallowed down a niggling tendril of propriety that whispered this was all just for show.

It could be real. If she was real with him. *Climb that last rung, Lennon.*

So she blurted out, "All I've ever wanted from you was a kiss."

A knot stuck at the base of her throat. She'd said it. Put her heart out there. And Ozzy hadn't flinched. Yet. He simply stared into her eyes. What was he thinking? That he'd chosen the wrong woman to act as a girlfriend? A woman who was supposed to fulfill her role then walk away. Just friends. *Nothing weird going on folks, look away.*

"Lemon, you mean so much to me." He bowed his forehead to hers. "I do want to kiss you."

Hello! Those feelings she'd tried to deny since arriving on the island and agreeing to be his fake girlfriend had never gone away. Because how to sever something that gave her such joy?

He traced a finger over her lips. Deciding? Was this going to be their first kiss? Oh yes! Yet he lingered, his skin barely touching hers. Why didn't he just kiss her?

No, he was making this slow. Romantic. Their first kiss would be a kiss to remember.

"I..." He stepped back and shoved his hands in his pockets.

Lennon's heart dropped. The sound of its splash in her gut felt audible.

"I don't know how to accept...*this* as something that could be real," he said. "I don't have that skill. And I thought I could change my thinking like you explained to me, that maybe this *was* the hot summer romance you wanted."

"You did?" Wow, that was... "Why didn't you say something?"

"I thought you were on the same track as me. That *I* was your hot summer romance."

"You are. You could be. I mean, you're not unlovable, Ozzy."

"You're starting to make me realize that. But. I'm still your brother's best friend. Lennon, I don't want to jeopardize losing the Hart family's love because I was stupid enough to think I could date you."

"But my parents approve. They were happy to hear we are dating."

"But we're not dating. Not for real. I've asked you to do something incredibly selfish on my part. Look at what happened with the online comments. Those were because of the things I've asked you to do. I don't deserve you, Lemon. And I won't continue to hurt you."

With that, Ozzy strode off toward the villa, leaving her standing at the edge of the beach where the thin sliver of moonlight seemed to dull and lose its glamour, reducing the water's surface to a darkness that translated to a shiver in Lennon's heart.

She touched her mouth. The heat of his fingertips remained. Yet instead of warming her it chilled. He didn't deserve her? That was the stupidest—

Of course, she did know his history with feeling unloved. But she'd always been kind and receptive to him. Hadn't refused him a thing. Had been open to whatever he suggested and hadn't thrown herself at him in desperation. Not that she would have. They'd both matured. This wasn't high school.

He'd thought *he* was her hot summer romance? Yes, please.

But really? If he cared so much about her and thought they'd been headed for romance, then why was it now so easy for him to step back and walk away? Just as he'd done all those years ago.

Lennon was mentally thrust back to prom night when she'd stood on the curb before him, eyes closed, heart pounding in expectation of a kiss—and then he'd said it couldn't happen. No kiss. She was not his girl. He didn't want to upset Harry. He didn't know how to love her. And he'd gotten in his friend's car and left her standing at the curb. Alone. Betrayed.

Lennon shook her head. And swore. A real swear word. How could she have been so stupid? To fall into the charm and allure of Ozzy Wilder all over again? As if she hadn't learned her lesson the first time around?

"Idiot."

Laughter from near the bonfire chilled her neck. She wanted to go home. Now.

If a guy could kick himself, Ozzy would do so. He'd messed up the opportunity for a kiss with Lemon. Big time. And he'd meant it when he'd said he thought *they* were the romance she had wanted to manifest. A woman wouldn't ask for a kiss if she wasn't in it for the romance. Would she?

But damn! The little family he did have he didn't want to lose. Sure, the Harts had said they were happy he was dating their daughter. But if they learned it had been a ruse, they wouldn't be so thrilled with him persuading Lemon to assist in the deception.

"Why are feelings so complicated?"

"You talking about my sister?" Harry strolled onto the balcony where Ozzy stood, leaning on the railing. "I saw the two of you walking. You looked like you're getting, uh, close. Are you two…?"

What Harry implied seemed like a lost dream. Or more truthfully, something he didn't deserve. Why had he, for even a moment, thought that he and Lemon were a couple?

"I don't know, man."

Yes, he did know. And that complicated things. Confused the heck out of him, actually. He and Lemon?

"I really like her, Harry. But every time I begin to think Lemon feels the same something inside grabs me and pulls me out of the dream."

"Maybe that's for the best."

Ozzy jerked his head up. His friend shrugged

and said, "It's not that I wouldn't want a friend to date my sister. It's just… You and Len? You had a chance before and screwed that up."

"What? What do you mean?"

"Oh, man, don't you remember? You hurt her on that prom night."

"I was…" He hadn't meant to hurt her. "That was a favor to you, Harry. You said your sister didn't have a date. I was a gentleman. I danced with her. I…"

When they'd paused and Lemon had stepped onto the curb to turn to him, he'd taken her hands and gazed into her beautiful eyes. Giddy had been putting her mood lightly. Only an hour earlier he'd whispered in her ear that she was his girl. Because he'd been in the moment, dancing with her, laughing with friends, toasting with some whisky-laced punch.

But then he'd remembered that he had taken Lemon on the date as a favor to Harry. His best friend. The Hart family had been so good to him. And if he started dating their daughter, he felt sure they'd disapprove. He'd be kicked out of his pseudo-family just as he'd been kicked out of his real family.

So he'd apologized to Lemon and told her he didn't know how to love someone because of the way he'd grown up. That they could never date.

Easier for her to hate him than for him to explain his complicated feelings about being abandoned.

When one of his friends had cruised by with a carload of girls and said they were headed to a keg party, Ozzy had joined them. It was an escape from the uncertainty of wanting to kiss her. He'd known Lemon would make the block and a half walk home okay.

"You didn't hear my sister crying after she'd walked home alone," Harry said now. "I should have never asked you to take her out."

Ozzy ran his hand over his hair. "But I didn't even…"

All I've ever wanted from you was a kiss.

He hadn't kissed her. He should have kissed her.

And now, was he doing it again? Refusing her his affection because…no one could ever love him. That mindset was so deeply ingrained in his bones that he—he had to climb up from it. Especially now that life seemed to be looking up romance-wise.

Or probably he was reading Lemon's reactions to him all wrong. A kiss was just a kiss. Right? Nothing more? A test to see…

"I didn't mean to hurt her," Ozzy offered. "I should have invited her along to the kegger, but she was wearing that pretty dress and the party was in a muddy field."

"She didn't want to go to the keg," Harry said defensively. "She had a huge crush on you then, and maybe..." Harry fisted his fingers before him and then punched the air. "Maybe she's still got one. I knew this faking being your girlfriend thing wasn't going to work."

Yeah, it had been an idiot move. Actually thinking he could fool the Cozy Closets CEO into believing he was a worthy candidate to buy the company? Simply because he had a girlfriend? That his borrowed family rubbed off certain values on him?

"It's done," Ozzy said. "We'll stop right now. If Miss Chastain is going to sell to me, she's already made up her mind, so it won't matter if Lemon and I keep up the fake."

"Yeah, but everyone here thinks the two of you are a couple. Your grandma?"

"I have to tell her the truth. It's been driving me mad since the day we started this."

"And here I thought it was Lennon who'd drive you mad. Guess I don't know my little sister as well as I thought." Harry slapped him across the back. "I'm sorry for putting you in that position back then."

"I've never told Lemon you asked me to take her out," Ozzy said. "The two of you mean too much to me. She should never know that."

"You're a good man, Ozzy. I think you and Len

should keep up with the fake until after the ceremony. We don't need a big upset to spoil our day."

"I would never do that to you. Yeah, we'll…" Ozzy sighed.

He'd made a mess of what should have been a simple business transaction. And he'd involved Lemon. Asked her to lie for him. That was the worst. Lower than low. He needed to apologize to her.

Hell, all he wanted to do was protect Lemon and give her everything that would make her happy. Because he really did care about her. And with every second that passed, he realized he may be in deeper emotionally than he could manage.

CHAPTER NINETEEN

In four hours Harry and Claire would say "I do." The Hart family would grow, welcoming the Andersons to their holiday gatherings. Lennon was excited for her brother. And for the fact that she could someday become an aunt. Thinking of which, she'd seen Ozzy coochie-cooing Carmel earlier. Her name was actually Cammi, but she still preferred Ozzy's moniker.

With a heavy sigh, Lennon plopped onto the chaise in Ozzy's closet. She wasn't going to change into full wedding gear until an hour beforehand, so for now it was cutoffs and a T-shirt.

Ozzy hadn't been in the room when she'd woken. Had he even been here at all last night? After their walk on the beach, she'd come inside, taken a shower and had crawled into bed. Sniffing back a few tears before falling asleep.

Now she turned the seashell she held over and over. A fairy steed's alicorn. That moment on the beach had been perfect. As had all the other moments they'd had to themselves. To get to know one another. To laugh over a tub of frosting. To share their dreams.

Until he'd ran away from their almost-kiss last night.

She dropped the seashell onto the chaise beside her and cupped her hands over her face. What was wrong with her? Was this still just a business transaction to him? Did he fully intend to introduce her to one of his friends after the wedding? To help her manifest that stupid summer romance? Why had she even posted about manifesting the romance? And her online silence had led her followers to believe it could be Ozzy. Not cool.

Lennon had thought she and Ozzy were starting to connect. That maybe they *were* the summer romance she had manifested. No. Ozzy was just another accessory, like the lemon diamond necklace, like all the stuff he'd bought for her since arriving.

If she were honest with herself, she didn't need a guy to feel wanted or to manifest a romance to help increase her clicks. While she'd taken a hit in her likes, with people accusing her of being fake, she had to agree she may be acting as desperate as Ozzy was. No one could fake romance. And not all manifestations came to fruition. She did not need a man to make her feel worthy or to boost her self-esteem. She'd come so far in performing for others and putting herself out there online.

No longer would she tell herself the story that she was not confident.

As for what was happening with Ozzy? It hadn't felt fake to her in those moments when they'd shared eye contact, hearts beating, breaths softly anticipating. Floating on the blue water under white caves with him, lost in a fantasyland. Racing across the sand and tumbling in one another's arms, laughing so hard their lungs had hurt. Being introduced to his favorite log. Somewhere along the line she'd forgotten her goal to find romance and had simply stumbled into it. Had become that woman confident enough to follow her heart.

Yet she was a fool to believe it might be real with Ozzy. She was only a tool to him, a means to get back his grandmother's company.

"I don't even want a romance now," she muttered, and flung herself backward to lie on the chaise, one arm stretched dramatically across her forehead. "I have failed to manifest."

And even if she stayed on after the wedding, she'd lost the will to seek a new man. Because there was only one man who meant something to her.

This was her brother's big day. She had to be there for Harry. Put on a smile and perform the pieces Claire had requested. Make it all look good. She needed to manifest mental strength.

The house bustled with the catering crew and the wedding planner's posse. Everyone had their job. Ozzy wandered through, avoiding collisions with determined-looking people in crisp white coats who were speaking in their earpieces. It was over the top, but Claire seemed pleased, so that was what mattered.

Dodging a duo carrying a table toward the outer doors, he slipped into the sunroom and found the person he was looking for.

"Grandma, thought I'd find you in here."

Eliza righted from fussing over the wedding cake that towered four layers high and burst with pale pink and white flowers dotted with silver and gold accents.

"I always marvel over the things you bake."

"Thank you, Oscar dear. You don't think it's too much?"

There were actual feathers bursting at the top in place of a traditional plastic bride and groom. Ozzy suspected that had been Claire's idea.

"Everyone is going to love it," he said. "But it doesn't matter what it looks like, it's how it tastes. And I do know that frosting..."

"You found the tub I left for you. Good boy."

He beamed in his grandmother's praise. "I

know how you work. Lemon thought it was good, too."

"Where is your girlfriend this morning? Enjoying her beauty rest before the busy day?"

"Lemon doesn't need beauty rest. She's gorgeous all the time."

Ozzy checked himself. Had he just said that? Without first thinking that he needed to put on an act? Yes, he had. Huh. Way to go, crazy emotional ride. He was on it, clinging with his fingernails.

He'd left Lemon early this morning after another stint sleeping in the closet. After he'd walked away from her on the beach, he couldn't bring himself to crawl into bed beside her. She'd been upset because he'd had to tell her the truth.

But had it been the truth? Did he seriously believe he could sacrifice a relationship with Lemon just to keep on the good side of her family?

All he'd wanted to do was kiss her!

"Lemon is..." He sighed and sat on a stool before the table that glittered with a silver fabric and real roses strewn here and there.

"Oh, Oscar." Eliza gave him a hug across his shoulders. "What is it, sweetie?"

"Grandma, I have to be honest with you. It doesn't feel right to continue this ruse. Nothing feels like it should. And my feelings for Lemon, especially, are confusing me."

"Oh dear, did you two break up?"

"No, it's not that. It's… Grandma, please don't be mad at me, but…" He swiped a hand over his face and shook his head. "We've been faking being a couple all week. For reasons that felt important to me. But ultimately, I've realized it was a stupid move. And the playacting may have hurt Lemon more than I could imagine."

Eliza stood back and nodded. No comment. And then… "I know, Oscar. I've suspected since the beginning."

"What?"

"Well, certainly I'd love it if the two of you were a real couple. But I could see it between the two of you. Trying for something that you both aren't willing to believe in. Lennon always seeming to direct you into hugging her. You giving her longing looks but only after she walked away. Why the fake? Was it for Lennon's stuff online? I know she's all about manifesting."

"It wasn't Lemon's idea. She came to Greece in search of romance. With someone who is *not* me. And I needed a quick image alteration so I would appear more of a normal, loving family sort of guy."

"Oh? But, Oscar, you are very loving. As for normal, who wants to be normal?"

Ozzy chuckled. "Good ole Grandma. The truth is, I've been trying to buy Cozy Closets. Specifically to get back the intellectual property that they stole from you."

"Oh? Well, I…" She smoothed a hand down her throat. "That's very noble of you, Oscar. That's quite a revelation."

For some reason, she didn't seem as surprised as he'd expected. Almost as if she'd known that was what he had been doing. Impossible.

"I was hoping to surprise you by handing over the company. Then you could do with it as you pleased. Things haven't gone as planned though."

"Amaris Chastain isn't deserving of the upgrade you could give her company."

He'd not thought of it like that, but… "How do you know Amaris?"

"Well, she's staying just down the hall from me."

Ozzy's jaw dropped open.

"Did you actually think you could hide her for days? I've been checking in on her. She thinks I'm staff. A housekeeper."

"Seriously? Grandma, what have you been up to?"

"I was curious about the *relative with the flu*—" she made air quotes "—so I had to find out the real story. Don't worry. She doesn't know me. Her mother worked with a much younger

Eliza Wilder, and I didn't tell her my name. I used my buttercream to get some info out of her. I don't believe she has any intention of selling to you." She placed a hand over his and gave it a squeeze. "She's taking advantage of your kindness, Oscar. You've got to cut that woman loose today."

"You learned all that with your frosting?" Ozzy laughed and shook his head. "Who would have thought my grandma would be so sneaky. But really, you think she won't sell?"

"It's a guess, but I'm rarely wrong when intuition strikes. It's not even about you and your supposed lack of family values or that risqué marketing campaign. Those are merely excuses. I know it's the rivalry between me and Sandra Chastain. There are things I never told you and… well. The Chastain family as a whole can't let it go. So we should wipe them from our concern. Not give them the time of day."

Things she hadn't told him? Dare he ask? She'd brushed it off. He wanted to know. Would that help him to ultimately win the company? Did she even want it?

"But you had a hand in everything Cozy Closets stands for, even today, Grandma. It was your original idea. How can you walk away from the chance to get it back?"

"It was tough those first few years. And I

admit I have carried a grudge against them. May have even influenced you to hate them, which troubles me deeply."

"Any animosity I hold toward Cozy Closets is entirely of my own making. So don't worry about that."

"Thanks, Oscar. But you know? Talking to Amaris made me rethink all of what I went through. I've moved on. I don't need to carry that anger. And what would I do with the company now? I'm an old woman!"

"You could sell it. Donate the money to charity. Or I could fold it into Wilder's Wardrobes."

"Oh, Oscar, I love you." She hugged him. A kiss to his forehead had always cheered him up. "You must know I appreciate the effort you put into trying to buy the company. I mean, making up the wild story of having a girlfriend just to convince them you're a family man? That's pretty crazy."

"It was. But…" This information would have been great to have *before* he'd asked Lemon to fool Chastain. But perhaps it wouldn't have come considering his grandma had said she'd reflected on it only since talking to Amaris. So he had been a catalyst of sorts to that realization. Still. "I've failed you."

"You've never failed me, Oscar. And I have always loved you. Always will. You're stuck with me. And you and Lennon? I can see she's good for you. You've just gotten lost in all the *stuff* this week. What does your heart want?"

Yes, what did it want? When he waded through the emotions of sudden desire and understanding, the misunderstandings and fear, and even cherishing every moment with Lemon, he knew the answer. "My heart seems to think that Lemon is the only woman for me. The only one I've ever wanted."

"Then you should go after what you want."

"But if something were to go wrong… Grandma, I love the Hart family. I don't want to mess up a good thing."

"Really? Because Angela mentioned how excited she was to learn the two of you are dating. Oscar. Dearest. I suspect that's not the real reason you're holding back."

She wasn't wrong. When Lemon had first arrived, he'd thought she could teach him how to be more free, not so uptight and open. When would he follow her lead and take, as Lemon would put it, what the universe wanted him to have?

"Ozzy!" Harry popped in, half dressed in tuxedo pants and an unbuttoned dress shirt. "I need your help, man."

Ozzy kissed his grandma on the head. "Thanks, Grandma. We will talk later about acquiring

Cozy Closets. It's not a done deal yet. Harry! Guess it's time I pull on my best man act, eh?"

"We have only a few hours before I walk down the aisle, and I am freaking out."

"Yeah?" Ozzy stretched an arm across his best friend's back. "Let's get you chilled."

Lennon followed the rush of bridesmaids swooping in and out of Harry and Claire's room. The room was a bustle of dresses, misplaced shoes, champagne, flowers, and even tears from Claire's mom. She hugged Mrs. Anderson and then dipped to tickle Carmel's toes. The baby wore a purple onesie to match the bridesmaids' dresses.

Claire stood before the floor-length mirror in a plush white robe. Beautiful thick curls cascaded around her head and down to her shoulders. One of her bridesmaids was testing which angle to pin on the rhinestone-bespangled veil.

"Lennon!" Claire waved at her in the mirror so she felt it was okay to step up and give her a careful side hug. Didn't want to mess her hair.

"I'm getting a sister today," Lennon said to her, feeling tears loosen at the corners of her eyes. "You make Harry so happy. I don't want to bug you too much because you've got enough going on, but I wanted to stop in and tell you I love you. And welcome to the family. Officially, that is."

Claire pulled her into a hug. "I love you, too.

We'll have to start making sister dates so we can get to know one another better. Of course, if you and Ozzy are a thing maybe we'll have another wedding soon?"

"You never know." The lump in her gut roiled. Harry could tell Claire about the fake on their honeymoon.

"Oh my god, Lennon, look at that necklace!" Claire tapped the heavy diamond at her neck. "It's so big! Did Ozzy give this to you?"

"Yes, he, uh..." Carp! This lying business hurt. "But it's just a—" Prop. She would be handing it over to him tomorrow morning when she booked a flight for Minnesota. The idea of staying on another week had lost its sparkle. She just wanted to go home and manifest a sulk.

She gave Claire another quick side-hug. "I'll see you when you're walking down the aisle, okay?"

"Yes, and would you check on Harry? I've heard he's nervous. He better not be thinking about changing his mind."

"Will do. And don't worry. Harry loves you madly, Claire. I think the veil should be tilted a little farther back."

The bride's friend, who had been standing aside, stepped up and shifted the veil. "Perfect," Claire declared.

Lennon made her way out of the room and

once in the kitchen she was handed flowers. By a man who epitomized Greek sexy, all olive skin and dark wavy hair and a killer white smile that could blind the sun.

"Uh." Lennon looked over the bouquet of daisies and yellow roses. Beautiful, but she wasn't sure what to do with it. The guests were starting to arrive. Was this…a wedding gift?

"I am Dimitri Athanas." He stretched out his arms as if waiting for a hug. Lennon took a step back. "Ozzy has told me about you. Or rather he suggested I may want to invite you around the island for a day."

"Oh? Oh." Heart kicking her chest hard, and then dropping, Lennon fought back tears while trying to paste on a smile. Ozzy had already contacted the potential date. And here he stood, looking like a billion dollars and smelling oh, so delicious.

So not ready for this. But wow. Was it the air on this island that forged such gorgeous men? Dimitri gave Ozzy a run for his money, and Ozzy was hands down stunning.

What *had* she manifested?

"Do not worry, I know the family is busy with the event. And you…" He looked her up and down, a slight wince tugging the corner of one of his eyes. "Perhaps you must prepare as well?"

She wore scruffy shorts and a T-shirt. Hadn't done her hair yet. Great first impression. Not.

But she didn't care. She hadn't the desire to date Dimitri. Not with her newly broken heart leaking sadness like a sinking boat.

"Thank you for the flowers, Dimitri. I, uh, I'm sure we'll find a chance to chat later." Unless she found a hole to crawl into and hide.

"I will make sure of it," he said with the most delicious Greek accent. Sexy. And—no, she couldn't even summon interest.

Nodding, she tucked the flowers against her chest and made a turn back down the hallway toward the bedrooms. Hoping upon hope that Ozzy wasn't in his bedroom because she needed a place to fall apart.

CHAPTER TWENTY

THE CEREMONY WAS PERFECT. The groom cried as the bride walked down the aisle—barefoot, both of them; so beachy. The bride blushed when, in the groom's vows, he promised to keep her happy, healthy and well-pleasured for all their lives. And Lennon played the entire wedding party out with the Bach concerto.

The wedding photos took hours while the guests milled about the house and pool, dining on hors d'oeuvres and champagne. During that time, Lennon had escaped to Ozzy's bedroom again with the excuse that she needed to freshen up her makeup. Happy tears. Mostly, she'd wanted to avoid anyone seeing her talking to Dimitri, who kept winking at her. Couldn't have anyone thinking she was two-timing her real boyfriend.

"Real," she muttered as she wandered back to the beach. "Far from it."

An early evening meal was served. And now, as the sun was dipping in the sky, the beach glittered and the waves lapped softly at the shore.

The band played the first dance to—naturally—a Taylor Swift song.

Lennon stood beside her mom, the two of them hugging, as they watched Harry dance with Claire beneath a disco ball, his focus on his new wife.

"So romantic," Angela Hart said. "Don't you think, Lennon?"

"A perfect summer romance," she said, feeling her heart play mutiny at a time when she should only be happy for her brother.

All this blatant romance was starting to make her itch. And every time she caught a glimpse of Ozzy he was either chatting to a guest or family member, or being tugged away for another bridal party photo op. And then her gaze would land on Dimitri. She had to tell him she wasn't interested.

Feeling all the love from her surrounding family, but also a little off-kilter because…where was *her* summer romance? The man who would stand beside her and give her a loving hug? She'd thought maybe she and Ozzy would dance because that's what a couple did, but even thinking about faking it any longer gave her a headache. It was over. Tomorrow they could go back to their separate lives and…

It had felt like a romance to her. A *great* summer romance.

"You going to dance with your boyfriend?" her mom asked.

"Soon." Lennon kissed her mom on the cheek. Fingers crossed, her parents would have a good laugh when the truth came out. "I'm going to get something cool to drink. Do you want anything?"

"I'm good. I'm going to find your dad. We haven't slow danced in a long time."

Lennon squeezed her mom's hand and then wove her way through the crowd, across the beach and to the edge of the house where the caterers served Eliza's cake and mixed drinks. "Ice water, please."

From behind, she felt a hand slide across her back and her skin prickled in anticipation. Thinking it was Ozzy, she turned with a smile, and… "Oh. Dimitri. I, uh…"

"I think you are avoiding me, Lennon from America. Ozzy said you were eager to meet someone while here. I'm sorry if I may have misunderstood him?"

Time to rip off the Band-Aid. "I was."

"Oh?"

"I'm so sorry, Dimitri. I'm sure you're a very nice man, but I've had a change of heart the last few days. Not sure I'm up for dating right now."

"Ah. It is because of Ozzy."

"No. I, uh, why do you say that?"

The man shrugged. "He speaks very highly

of you. I was thinking to myself during the ceremony: why would he want to hook up a friend with someone he cares about so much?"

"Oh. Well." Really? Did a man walk away from the woman he cared about over a kiss?

"I understand." Dmitri leaned in and kissed her cheek. "It is my loss. You are talented and beautiful, Lennon Hart. I do not know you, but I think you and Ozzy are a good pair."

Yeah, that ship had sailed. Or rather, sunk.

"I feel quite awful that you came here and spent all this time at a stranger's wedding and for what?"

"I got to spend the day with an amazing family and share wonderful food and drinks."

"Thank you for being so understanding. You should stick around for the fireworks. They're setting them off after the dance."

"I will. And maybe we will dance before the night is over?"

"I'd like that."

Relief washed over Lennon as Dimitri strolled away. That hadn't been as difficult as she'd been expecting. Ozzy spoke highly of her? Only because she was a tool that, at least she hoped, got him exactly what he wanted—Cozy Closets. Otherwise, this second trip down heartbreak lane would have been in vain.

Ice water in hand, she steered away from the

spinning disco ball flashes and found a semiquiet spot on a boulder nestled at beach edge. Checking her phone, she would not post any wedding photos. It wouldn't be polite without permission from everyone in every shot, and that was too much work. But she had gotten a great one of Harry and Claire dancing. Their faces had been blocked by a disco ball. She posted it along with the caption: *True love sparkles.*

Scrolling to her stats, she saw her comments and—ouch. Those were some nasty comments.

I found her summer romance man. He's a billionaire! Oscar Wilder of Wilder's Wardrobes.

How did she manage that? She's not that pretty.

Apparently, he's a good friend of her brother's.

She's scamming us. Manifesting romance? How about fake it for the follows. I'm out of here.

I can't believe she would do that to us, guys.

I'm sure it's legit. She'll respond. Right, Lennon?

Lennon pressed the phone to her forehead. A rapid spill of swear words came out as harsh whispers. She deserved every angry post. What a fake she had become. And all because she'd been trying to help out a friend.

Two arguing voices prompted her to scan the beach. The guests were all eating, laughing and chatting near the dance floor. Lennon's eyes veered to the back of the villa. Amaris, suitcase in one hand, was talking to—

"Eliza? Oh no."

Lennon hustled across the sand. "If they learn who each other are, this is not going to be good."

"You crazy people scammed me!" Amaris hissed loudly. She wobbled, using the extended suitcase handle as a makeshift crutch.

"Amaris." Lennon approached the two women. "We should get you sitting. It's not good to be standing on your ankle—"

"Screw my ankle. I'm fine," she barked. Lennon stepped back from her vehemence. "I can't believe she was sneaking in and spying on me!"

Lennon looked to Eliza, who offered a helpless shrug.

"You and my dad—" Amaris shook a finger at Eliza, but then shook her head. "I can't even talk to you. You're a wicked woman. And you!" The CEO turned her phone toward Lennon, and she saw it was open to her TikTok page. "Are you even Mr. Wilder's girlfriend?"

Lennon swallowed. The lie had become too

big. How to save what little dignity she had remaining? If she'd ever had any in the first place.

Eliza tugged Lennon close, putting an arm around her shoulders. "Of course, she is. And she's about the sweetest person you'll ever meet. But it shouldn't matter to you if Oscar has a relationship, is married with children, or a bachelor who has a solid brand and makes billions because of it. Cozy Closets would be in the best hands if he owned it, and you know it."

Amaris lifted her nose, sneering. "Well. If he offered more…"

"Absolutely not," Eliza said.

Lennon gaped at her. Ozzy wanted Cozy Closets for a reason. And if Eliza stopped that from happening he would be devastated.

"Take your tired old closets and do what you want with them," Eliza spat. "I'll call the driver to pick you up. You've overstayed your welcome, Chastain."

"Don't bother. A cab is on the way."

Taking Lennon's hand, Eliza tugged her around the side of the house, out of the wedding party's view and to the side entrance. Once there, she stopped and gave Lennon a hug. "Thank you for not interfering, Lennon. I needed to have words with that woman. Though, it wasn't as satisfying as I'd hoped. It should have been Sandra I had words with, not her daughter."

"Can I ask what she meant when she started to say something about you and her dad?" Lennon cringed. Now that she'd spoken the words, she could guess.

Eliza pressed a hand to the pearls circling her neck. "That was a long time ago."

"Did you..." How to have such a conversation with a woman she had thought to be a sweet little old lady who could do no wrong? "Was *that* the reason you were kicked out of Cozy Closets?"

With a heavy sigh, Eliza nodded. "You must never tell Oscar his grandmother had an affair with another woman's husband. Promise me?"

Brain bursting with the salacious information, Lennon could only nod. Extremely good reason to want to force a partner out of a company. And keeping it a secret from Ozzy felt paramount. It would ruin his opinion of his grandmother, who could do no wrong in his eyes.

"It was a long time ago," Lennon found herself saying as a means to agreeing to keep the secret. "But, Eliza, now Ozzy will never be able to buy Cozy Closets."

"Oh, dearest, I know he was only doing it for me. And you know? I don't want anything to do with that company."

"But it was your idea to create the company. Ozzy said it was *all* your idea. That Sandra was just the one with the money."

Eliza took her hands. "True. But it's been decades. I've found my place in the world. And now that you've learned what a sordid woman I am..."

The whole ruse had been so Ozzy could show his grandma his love.

"I wasn't thinking that, Eliza."

"I was in a bad place after my husband's death. Needed comfort. The affair just happened. It was wrong. I deserved to be ousted from Cozy. And you know? Having it back in hand would feel more like a burden than a gift. I've moved on. I hadn't realized Oscar was set on acquiring the company as a gift to me. Oh. I don't want to break the boy's heart. He's been through so much already. Oh dear, I really have bungled things, haven't I?"

"Maybe a bit."

"Will you talk to Oscar for me?"

"Me?" How to break it to her that she and Ozzy were not even a couple?

"Oh, how can I ask that? It's my responsibility to clear things up with my grandson. Thank you for helping Oscar this week, dearest. Your ruse was really quite something."

"Uh, sure."

Eliza went inside, leaving Lennon stunned that she and Ozzy had not even convinced her for one moment. Really? So all this time? Why hadn't she said anything? And to know who Amaris was? She'd had an affair with Amaris Chastain's dad? Her former partner's husband?

Well, well, Eliza Wilder had some wild in her after all.

If Eliza would have said something to Ozzy right away…

They may have never had this week of pretending to date. A week that, despite its falseness, had sunk into Lennon's being, her very soul. But he didn't feel the same about her as she did him.

So it was to be another moment where she stood on the curb, wondering if he would kiss her. And this time she knew he would not.

As far as she was concerned, the sun better set soon. Her performance was scheduled when the band took a break, which was soon. She could escape the beach party after that. Crying in her room felt most appropriate.

CHAPTER TWENTY-ONE

After Lennon's performance during the band's break, she put away her violin and veered toward the champagne table. That navigation took far too long as family and friends accosted her every few steps. Finally, she held a goblet in each hand.

Lennon glanced around to spy Ozzy talking to Dimitri. She ducked behind a column wrapped with gauzy white chiffon. Carp. The match would have been exactly what she'd wanted had it happened a day or two after arriving here in Greece. But now? So much had changed in her heart.

Lennon shook her head. She was over the whole quest for a summer romance. The last rung in her self-confidence ladder? So much for daring to ask for what she wanted, to manifesting romance. Her heart had been broken once again by the longing love she held for Ozzy. Sure, he'd *said* he wanted to kiss her, too, but it hadn't been enough, *she* hadn't been enough, for him to actually do it.

Would she never learn?

All of a sudden Ozzy turned and made eye contact with her. That sexy smile. A lift of his champagne glass for a toast across the way. She lifted hers, but her smile didn't come. When he started toward her, her erratic heartbeats protested. *No, you don't want to do this near a crowd. Turn and run!*

As she turned, Ozzy's hand slid across her back and he came around to block her escape. "We need to talk, Lemon."

Had Dimitri complained to him? He'd come to a stranger's wedding to meet a woman and had been soundly rejected? The guy had actually seemed okay with hanging around and partying when she'd spoken to him, so it had to be something about her and Ozzy. But what was left to say? They both knew this had been a business agreement. Fake it so he could win the deal. And now he wasn't even going to win the deal. The whole thing had been pointless.

Eliza had an affair with Sandra Chastain's husband, and she couldn't tell Ozzy. Oh, this tangled web!

"If it's about the Cozy Closets deal, I'm sorry," she said.

"It's not that. I know Amaris isn't going to sell. Grandma told me she had words with her."

"Oh? What sort of words?"

"It's that long-held rift between Sandra Chastain and my grandma. I don't know why it's so deep, but, well, I don't know what to do anymore, Lemon. I thought Grandma would appreciate getting Cozy Closets back."

"Maybe you just need to step back from it for a few days."

"I can't even think about that right now. It's us, Lemon, I—"

"It's okay. The fake is over tonight. We tried our best. You don't need to pretend anymore."

"That's the thing. I'm not pretending, Lemon. I'm not sure I have been at any moment since you arrived."

"Give it up, Ozzy. I'm not going to ask you to hook me up with a friend either. I told Dimitri no. I've given up on romance."

"Lemon." He took her by the shoulder, and a little champagne spilled from one of the goblets. "Since you've arrived, you've made me see things much clearer. I am loved. I do have a family."

"Of course, you do. My family adores you. And my parents were thrilled when I told them we were dating. They would never abandon you like your—" Shoot. "I'm sorry."

"I realize that now. I really do. It may take a while for Harry to come around if we were to—I mean… So maybe…"

A woman wielding a champagne bottle and

wearing a silky purple bridesmaid dress fluttered over and hooked her arm with Ozzy's arm. "We're needed on the dance floor, best man. The wedding party is dancing."

"I, uh…" Ozzy winced. Looked at Lennon.

She shrugged. "You'd better go. Claire has the whole evening planned to the very last detail. You wouldn't want to upset the bride."

"Come on. It'll just take a few minutes." The bridesmaid tugged Ozzy, who reluctantly followed.

Lennon waved as the man was led away. "Good talk," she muttered. Then turned to resume her mission to find a quiet place to drink herself to oblivion.

She headed away from the party and wandered toward a few chaise longues. Chose one and sat.

Tilting her head against the chaise, she closed her eyes. Ozzy now realized her family loved him? Good for him. It was a real love. He deserved that second son designation.

As for them being the hot summer romance?

Lennon clasped both the champagne goblets, holding them one on each thigh. Time to drown her sorrows. Her heart was defeated. This might be her bottom. She'd allowed her heart to once again feel something for Ozzy.

It hadn't been real in high school. Just an infatuation.

"Not true," she said to the bubbling concoctions waiting to be imbibed.

She may have been in love with the image, the *idea* of Ozzy in high school, but now she'd gotten to know him. And she knew who he was and what he wanted and how he treated those in his world. So much to adore about the man.

Yet he could never be hers. That kiss she'd always wanted would never come.

What had she thought to do? Manifest a summer romance with a *billionaire*? She'd gotten great content, but her followers had seen through her. She deserved the backlash. Could she turn it around and show them that judging others reflected on their own insecurities? No, she would not be so cruel, even to faceless followers she didn't know. Likes and follows meant nothing. They no longer provided validation. They never had. She'd gotten real validation from Ozzy… until she had not.

Bringing the champagne goblets together in a ting, she moved them to her mouth. To sip from both at the same time? Not a logistical possibility. Tilt one back in a swallow? Then chug the other? Unladylike, but if she intended to wallow in misery, it was the only way to go.

Pressing the cool glass rim to her lips, she closed her eyes at the tingle of bubbles striking her nose. *Do it quick.*

"Lemon!"

Before the alcohol hit her tongue, Ozzy plunged to her side in the sand and grabbed both glasses from her. "I don't think so, Lemondrop."

Lennon slammed her arms across her chest and gave him a thorough pout. "You're not the boss of me."

"Oh. So we're acting like children now?"

He tossed the contents of the goblets onto the sand and set the empties on a nearby table then stood over her, hands on his hips. Like some disapproving adult. Nothing whatsoever attractive about a man who hijacks a girl's only means to obliterating her heartbreak in an ocean of champagne.

"Go back to the wedding. It's your affair. You need to oversee the whole thing."

"Yeah? Well, it's your brother. You should be sharing in all that love and happiness foolishness."

"Love is not foolish."

Ozzy sat on the end of the chaise near her legs, so she pulled them up and put her arms around them.

"No, it's not," he said. "Were you actually looking to get drunk?"

"Maybe. It's a party. That's what people do."

"Not you."

"You think you know me so well?"

"Lemon, what's with the attitude? I've been trying to find a few minutes alone with you all day and you keep avoiding me. At first I thought it was because you wanted to get to know Dimitri, but then I talked to him and he told me you rejected him."

"I didn't reject him. He's a very handsome man. I just..." Oh! Why could he not see what she thought was so blaring and *right there* in between the two of them? "Ten minutes ago you told me you thought *we* were the hot summer romance. And that you were seeing yourself surrounded by family."

"I do and I did. I love the Harts. And... I'm getting such mixed signals from you."

"We were *faking* it, Ozzy."

"Were we? Because honestly? I wasn't."

She turned her head to the side to hide her wince. If tears started, she would scream because she didn't want him to see her vulnerable.

"I'm sorry, Lemon. What's bugging me is not my panic over losing your family if we started to date. It's because I didn't kiss you last night." He bowed to meet her gaze. "Yes, I realize now that I've hurt you again. At prom I... I said those things in order to make sure you would stop crushing on me. But in that moment? I so wanted to kiss you. I crushed on you, too, Lemon."

A gape was all she could manage.

"It had to be done. That stupid teenager thought hurting you would stop it all cold. Because, well…"

"I know you carry a belief that no one will ever—Well. I know how you feel about being loved, Ozzy. But don't worry. The Hart family will always love you."

He bent and kissed her knee. "All my life I've carried this heavy burden about being unlovable. Blame it on my parents. I mean, they were there for me until I was ten. Mostly. But I'm a grown man now. And much as that shaped me, I feel like something has shifted in me this week."

"Like what? Is it your grandma? It's nice having her here with you, I know that. I'm so glad she's accepted your offer to move in."

"I love Grandma. She's always been there for me. But, Lemon…"

He stroked the hair along her face and Lennon inhaled, pulling up the bravery required to face him, to listen, and not judge anymore. He was putting himself out there, and she wanted to respect that.

"Lemon," he said again. He tilted his head back, closed his eyes, then nodded. When he looked at her, his eyes flickered from the distant lights on the beach. "I should have kissed you at prom."

Yes, he should have. But what then? Would that

have changed her life? Would she be in a different position today? Would they have dated? Broken up? Maybe never spoken to one another again for the awkwardness of their connection to Harry?

"Stand up." He stood and took her hand. Walking her out onto the beach until they reached a slope, he stopped her, then stepped down the incline. "Okay. Perfect. This is kind of how it was back then. You were standing on the curb."

"You remember that?"

"Of course. I remember it all, Lemon. You wore a blue dress about the color you're wearing now. I remember thinking how much I liked it because it was the same color as my skateboard."

"Blue is my favorite color."

"It's mine, too. See, we have stuff in common."

"Favorite color does not make for a..." Lasting relationship. "It hasn't even been a week. Despite the fun we've had playacting at a couple, you don't even know me."

"Oh yeah?" He shrugged. "I know you like blue."

She gave him an incredulous tilt of her head.

"I know you are a talented violin player whose favorite composer is Paganini." He held up a hand and started ticking off fingers. "I know you love buttercream and will eat it like it's going out of style. No matter the consequences." He winked at her. "I know that you are an introvert with extrovert tendencies when you're around people you know. But forget strangers. You'd prefer they approach you to start a conversation as opposed to vice versa."

He was not wrong. So far.

"I know you genuinely care about people. That if your heart isn't in a project, then you'd rather not do it. You see the best in people before they even know it themselves. Like you saw the good parts in me. And…you made me believe in those good parts, Lemon."

He'd been paying attention to her this whole time.

"And I also know that this weird quest for a romance to prove to yourself that you've got confidence is just a distraction from you wanting to heal a heart that you've always felt was broken. I'm sorry that I was the one to break your heart, Lemon."

She couldn't find words. Now that the apology was out there, she wished he would take it back. He didn't need to apologize for acting out of a fear instilled from lacking love.

"I know a lot about you, too," she said. Because two should play this game. "I know you wear your heart on your sleeve. Your kindness is the first thing to rise before judgment or indifference. You are trustworthy. I know you love children. I mean, you and Carmel? What is that about?"

He shrugged. "I do love kids."

"Her name is Cammi, but I think we should stick with Carmel. If I had heard you babysat when we were younger, I might never have believed it. But now? Holding a baby suits you. And you know what else I know about you?"

"What's that?"

"That you would die for Harry."

"Almost did that one time we were skiing in Telluride."

Harry had told the whole family how Ozzy had skied in front of him, redirecting his course from an avalanche, and in the process Ozzy had wiped out and his legs had been buried to the thighs. A rescue team had to dig him out.

"You do know me," he said. "That means something to me. We go deep, Lemon."

"We do," she said with awe. Believing it for the first time.

She and Ozzy had been walking around and near one another for a long time. When had they finally crashed into one another? Of course they'd been a little discombobulated, unsure how to approach the other. Faking it had allowed them to finally turn and face one another.

"As for prom night." He stepped closer. "We

were standing at the curb, and I knew it was a moment for a kiss. You even closed your eyes."

Lennon blushed. It was sweet that he remembered, but also a little cringey in that he was replaying one of her most heart-wrenching moments.

"But the thoughts that went through my head at the time?" he continued. "I wanted to kiss you, Lemon."

She stopped herself from saying "You did?" Really? He'd wanted a kiss as much as her?

"But a bigger part of me was like 'You can't kiss your best friend's sister. Don't lose the one family you still have!'"

Fair enough. And she'd granted him that excuse over the years as a means to soften her own heartbreak.

"But you've helped me to see through that belief I told myself. It was wrong. I am loved. I do have family."

"I'm so glad you can see that, Ozzy. I want nothing more for you than such happiness."

"And you know what else I've realized?"

He stepped closer. Lennon's breath hushed out. The water glittered behind him. Stars actually blinked as if lighting a surreal stage. Standing on the incline, Ozzy's eyes were level with hers. It was as though she stood on the curb, hope in her heart. And he stood on the street, the boy she had lost her heart to. The guy who had given her butterflies. Then.

And now.

"I now know, Lemon, that I don't ever again want to pass up the opportunity to kiss you."

CHAPTER TWENTY-TWO

HAD SHE HEARD Ozzy correctly? Had he just…

So many thoughts raced through Lennon's head, crashing into one another and screaming for voice or a listen or even a reconsideration. But she didn't want to listen to any of that noise right now. Because Ozzy stood before her. Face-to-face. Dreamy star-glinting eyes locked on hers. Mouth speaking words she'd never thought to hear.

It felt genuine. Real. As if she had manifested this moment. And maybe she had. Maybe, just maybe, life was happening the way it wanted to.

"Lemon," he whispered. It wasn't a question, or a prompt. Just a statement.

Ozzy moved in, their faces closing the distance.

Heartbeats doing a wild dance, Lennon closed her eyes. Somewhere down the beach the band played a soft accompaniment to her giddy free-style. And in the sky a flash of brilliant fireworks sparked *oohs* and *aahs* from the wedding party.

Their lips connected. A long-awaited touch. Wanted. Desired. The prize she'd dreamed of was finally hers.

Ozzy slid his hand along her jaw. Her entire being tittered joyfully and her body tilted forward. His fingers dived into her hair as his palm moved along her skin and hair and cupped the back of her head. Hand fluttering, she reached and tried to anchor herself as the incredible kiss buoyed her. If her feet left the ground, she would not be surprised.

Hand clutching the front of his open dress shirt, she curled her fingers inside against his warm, steely-hard chest. He moved his mouth against hers, fitting more perfectly, finding his place.

Welcome, she thought. *This is where you belong.*

You deserve all the love, Ozzy.

"Lemon," he muttered in a rough growl as he turned his head and refocused their kiss.

His voice owned her. Did things to her insides. To her atoms and molecules. It permeated all bits, finding a place it might never vacate. He opened her mouth with his tongue. She matched his steps, quickly learning their unique dance. One of his hands slid up her back, coaxing her chest against his. Yes. Closer. She removed her hand from his shirt and wrapped both arms up and around his neck. His hair tickled between her fingers, soft and graspable. She held him there in the kiss.

The kiss.

The moment she had dreamed of had manifested. Nothing had ever felt so right. At last, the universe smiled upon her.

High above them fireworks lit up the sky. Startled, she jerked out of the kiss because Ozzy looked up but then quickly back to her. His smile had undone her for so long now all she could do was nod in agreement. As did he. They'd kissed.

Kissed!

He took her hand. "Let's go inside and watch the fireworks from my room."

"Yes." Anywhere with him. Even to his bedroom where she expected the kissing to resume and clothes to be torn away and naked limbs to tangle. "I'm glad that kiss took so long to happen," she said as they made haste toward the balcony connected to his bedroom.

Once at the door to his room, he pulled her into his embrace and kissed her again. The wait had been worth it. Now, they were truly ready to welcome one another into their respective lives.

"I think you're right, Lemon. We weren't ready for this when we were teens. Now?"

"Now?"

"Like I said, I don't ever want to pass up the chance to kiss you, Lemon. Every day."

If she didn't get this man into bed right now, someone from the wedding party might come looking for them. This best man had fulfilled his duties to the groom for tonight.

Now, he was all hers.

In the middle of the night, they lay in bed, naked, bodies hugging. Ozzy's sea scent merged with Lennon's buttercream parfum—she'd gotten some in her hair at some point during the festivities. Despite the wedding party still celebrating outside, they'd found a peaceful oasis away from it all. Here on this massive bed, curled against one another. Nothing felt better.

"There's a boat on the water," Lennon noted.

"That's the wedding party. I've got security keeping an eye on everyone. I'm not worried."

"Then I'm not either." She turned and snuggled her breasts against his chest. Her fingers found their place tucked in the ridges formed by his abs. Finally, she'd touched him. Everywhere. "Tell me this isn't just one night?"

"This isn't just one night, Lemon." He kissed her deeply. They'd created a new language between the two of them. One of softness and then rushed, wanting hunger. Of hard, deep kisses that ended in fluttering brushes of skin. "I've been lying here trying to figure how I can convince you to stay the summer."

"I have stumbled into a hot summer romance. Would be a shame to walk away now." She kissed his shoulder and snuggled in. "It occurred to me that we don't have to tell my parents or the rest of the crew that we're not a couple."

"Saved by a kiss on the beach?"

"I'll probably tell Mom the whole story. She'll laugh about it and then she'll hug me. Both my parents adore you."

"There's something about the Hart family that I just can't stay away from. Will you stay the summer?"

"I would love to."

"Will the flower shop miss you?"

"Do I care?"

"And you can do your online thing anywhere."

"Yeah, about that. I feel like a break is needed. Maybe a month or two of lazing on the beach. Just focusing on myself. And you."

"Yachting with me?"

"And scuba diving in the Blue Caves."

"Driving Grandma into town for shopping."

"It all sounds delicious."

He licked her shoulder. "You're the delicious one, Lemon." He tapped the necklace, the big heavy diamond cradled in her clavicle. "When I bought this, I think that teenager standing before you at the curb popped up and said 'Just do it. Show her how you feel. Maybe she'll like you.'"

"I loved that guy. And, well, this might sound too early or quick to say but—"

"I love you," he rushed to say.

Lemon nodded and snuggled into his embrace. "I love you, too."

Ozzy and Lemon's hot summer romance had just begun.

EPILOGUE

Hey, Manifesteers!

I've been quiet awhile because I wanted to think things through before speaking to all of you. I love you and appreciate that you take a few moments out of your day to check my reels. And I've heard from so many of you that you've manifested your dreams. Way to go!

I know others were shocked and saddened to believe that I may have been deceiving you during my stay in Greece. I went there for my brother's wedding, but also, I wanted to manifest romance. I tried. Then you all thought Ozzy was the guy I'd manifested. And you didn't believe it. Well guess what? I didn't believe it either. Honestly, Ozzy asked me to play his girlfriend for a certain situation, so I agreed to help a friend. But in truth? Something happened. We've known each other for years, and yes, I had a crush on him when I was in high school. Who knew he also had a crush on me?

Well, all of this to say, Ozzy and I are now an

official couple. We realized that we both love one another and couldn't imagine spending a day apart. So I actually did manifest him.

I'm going to take a break from my channel to enjoy every minute with my guy. Check back in the new year. I love you all!

OCTOBER LEAVES UNTETHERED themselves from the trees and fluttered through the air, gathering on the sidewalk that edged the seventeenth-century brick building in the 6th arrondissement of Paris. Ozzy owned the whole building. The entire top floor was his. Half of the floor just beneath that had been renovated, and Eliza had moved in a few weeks ago. Utterly thrilled with her own space in Paris, the woman spent her days walking the city and exploring. And sometimes she even invited Lennon to join her. But Lennon had already noticed a certain man who lived across the street, whose twinkling eyes would brighten when Eliza stepped out. She'd seen them walking arm in arm last night.

Setting a bag of macarons on the countertop—her latest obsession—Lennon knew that Ozzy was in his office. It wasn't yet noon, and she never bothered him when he was working. It gave her opportunity to do some city exploring in the mornings. But she preferred the afternoons and evenings when Ozzy would take her out on the town.

The city of love certainly hadn't been misnamed. Since moving to Paris Lennon had ended the lease on her apartment in Tangle Lake, said goodbye to Hanson's Flowers, and…she wasn't posting as much on TikTok because she didn't have the time. Or the desire. Truly, she had gotten a dopamine kick from every like and follow.

Now she didn't need that. She had the real thing. Love.

Ozzy covered all expenses and he enjoyed buying her clothes, and she'd ruled out more jewelry. The necklace was more than enough for Lennon Hart from small-town Minnesota. She didn't do bling. But those red-soled shoes? Yes, please. They were perfect for when they went to the Opera.

But not working wasn't her thing, so she had applied for an English-teaching job and when her contact at the school learned she played the violin, he mentioned they were looking for an English-speaking music instructor to teach expats a few days a week. She started next month.

"There you are!"

Lennon spun as Ozzy lifted her. Crushing a kiss against her mouth, he carried her over to the floor-to-ceiling window and set her down. "There." He pointed across the city to a distant speck of a building. "The Sacré-Coeur in Montmartre. Want to walk there?"

"Always *yes* to anything and everything in Paris. Are there macaron shops along the way?"

"If not, we'll find one." He kissed her forehead and pulled her into a hug. "I love you, Lemondrop."

"I love you, too, honeybun."

"Go grab a jacket. I'll meet you down at the curb."

Ozzy took off, while Lennon rushed back to their bedroom for a jacket. *Their* bedroom. In *their* home. This was real. The ultimate manifestation. She looked forward to spending the rest of her life with Ozzy Wilder.

Tugging on her jacket, she rushed out to the stairs and skipped down. Outside, Ozzy stood on the cobblestone street, waiting for her. It had become their thing. She was usually behind by a bit when they went out, searching for a coat or her phone so he went ahead. And positioned himself right *there*.

Lennon stopped at the edge of the curb. The only man she'd ever loved smiled at her.

And then he kissed her.

* * * * *

If you enjoyed this story, check out these other great reads from Michele Renae

Match Made in Seville
Reunion with Her Highland Rival
Jet-Set Nights with Her Enemy
Billion-Dollar Nights in the Castle

All available now!

Get up to 4 Free Books!

We'll send you 2 free books from each series you try PLUS a free Mystery Gift.

Both the **Harlequin® Historical** and **Harlequin® Romance** series feature compelling novels filled with emotion and simmering romance.

YES! Please send me 2 FREE novels from the Harlequin Historical or Harlequin Romance series and my FREE Mystery Gift (gift is worth about $10 retail). I may cancel anytime by emailing ReaderServiceInfo@Harlequin.com or by calling 1-800-873-8635. If I don't cancel, I will receive 5 new Harlequin Historical books every month and be billed just $6.39 each in the U.S. or $7.19 each in Canada, or 4 new Harlequin Romance Larger-Print books every month and be billed just $7.19 each in the U.S. or $7.99 each in Canada, a savings of 20% off the cover price. It's quite a bargain! Shipping and handling is just 75¢ per book in the U.S. and $1.75 per book in Canada.* I understand that accepting the free books and gift places me under no obligation to buy anything—they are mine to keep for free no matter what I decide.

Choose one: ☐ Harlequin Historical (246/349 BPA G3CD) ☐ Harlequin Romance Larger-Print (119/319 BPA G3CD) ☐ Or Try Both! (246/349 & 119/319 BPA G3CE)

Name (please print)

Address Apt. #

City State/Province Zip/Postal Code

Email: Please check this box ☐ if you would like to receive newsletters and promotional emails from Harlequin Enterprises ULC and its affiliates. You can unsubscribe anytime.

Mail to the **Harlequin Reader Service:**
IN U.S.A.: P.O. Box 1341, Buffalo, NY 14240-8531
IN CANADA: P.O. Box 603, Fort Erie, Ontario L2A 5X3

Want to explore our other series or interested in ebooks? Visit www.ReaderService.com or call 1-800-873-8635.

*Terms and prices subject to change without notice. Prices do not include sales taxes, which will be charged (if applicable) based on your state or country of residence. Canadian residents will be charged applicable taxes. Offer not valid in Quebec. This offer is limited to one order per household. Books received may not be as shown. Not valid for current subscribers to the Harlequin Historical or Harlequin Romance series. All orders subject to approval. Credit or debit balances in a customer's account(s) may be offset by any other outstanding balance owed by or to the customer. Please allow 4 to 6 weeks for delivery. Offer available while quantities last.

Your Privacy — Your information is being collected by Harlequin Enterprises ULC, operating as Harlequin Reader Service. For a complete summary of the information we collect, how we use this information and to whom it is disclosed, please visit our privacy notice located at https://corporate.harlequin.com/privacy-notice. Notice to California Residents—Under California law, you have specific rights to control and access your data. For more information on these rights and how to exercise them, visit https://corporate.harlequin.com/california-privacy. For additional information for residents of other U.S. states that provide their residents with certain rights with respect to personal data, visit https://corporate.harlequin.com/other-state-residents-privacy-rights.

HHHRLP2603